Catch Me, Cowboy

Catch Me, Cowboy

A Copper Mountain Rodeo Romance

Jeannie Watt

TULE
PUBLISHING

Chapter One

S HELBY O'CONNOR HEARD gravel crunch under tires on the opposite side of the barn, but didn't take her eyes off the horse circling her in the round pen. If she broke focus, so would the young gelding, and now that she'd made a small amount of headway in the respect department, she wasn't stopping. She gently slapped the coils of rope she held against her thigh and waved a hand to urge the horse to trot faster.

A truck door slammed and boots hit the ground.

Please be UPS.

If it wasn't, she could handle it.

The round pen was set up behind the barn, to keep the horses from being distracted while Shelby worked them, but unfortunately that also kept her from seeing who'd just driven in to the Forty-Six Ranch. Just because she'd gotten a couple of heads up texts early that morning informing her Ty Harding was back in town, it didn't mean he'd come to see her. Why would he? She'd made her feelings clear as glass when he'd left four years ago.

Shelby raised her hand and the gelding flicked an ear and shot a look at her out of one eye as he trotted around the perimeter of the pen, a sign he was starting to focus on her instead of escape.

Finally. Bueno Macho was a stubborn boy.

She took a couple of backward steps, dropping her arms to her side, relaxing her posture. The horse immediately slowed to a walk and then halted. He turned to face her, ears pricked forward. Full focus and a good stopping point—although, to be honest, Shelby was quitting because her focus was slipping. She slowly walked up to the horse, extending a hand and waiting until the horse bumped it with his nose.

"You did good." She rubbed the gelding's forehead before snapping the lead rope onto the halter and starting toward the gate, her heart thumping just a little harder as she crossed the sandy pen.

Moment of reckoning. Who is our mystery guest today?

Package delivery guy? Some lost soul looking for the nearly invisible turn-off to the River Road? Or...

Ty.

Her heart slammed against her ribs at the sight of the man who'd once been her whole world, leaning against his truck, the late morning sun behind him, looking every inch the cowboy he was. Dark hair escaped from beneath his Resistol and, even though the brim shaded his face, she could see his features were harder, more sculpted than before. Four years had changed him, but it had not dulled her reaction to him. Part of her wanted to rush into his arms, as she would have done before he'd so easily abandoned her, and another part wanted to smack him. Hard. Fortunately for both of them, the sane part of her prevailed, although it was a battle, and she kept her expression carefully distant as she crossed the drive.

"Shelby."

"You're back." She spoke on a flat note, as if her heart wasn't beating a mile a minute—which it shouldn't be.

They'd tried to make a go of it once. Failed. If he was back to make nice so they could live together in the same community…fine. She wasn't looking forward to it, but, hey…free country and all that.

"I am." He shifted his weight, hooking a thumb in his belt, a sure sign he wasn't as certain of himself as he appeared.

But even when Ty wasn't sure of himself, he was a formidable opponent. She knew from the confrontations they'd had when he'd asked her to come with him on the road. As if she could just leave grad school, her grandfather, and go. Right. It would have been easier for him to give up saddle bronc, or to ride only in the Montana Circuit instead of chasing the big titles. But no.

"And…?"

Again she tried to sound polite, yet distant, as if he were an acquaintance who'd stopped by for an unknown reason. As if he hadn't knocked her heart around, but good.

He shrugged, those gray-blue eyes of his holding her, causing her to lift her chin as she came closer. Ty was tall for a bronc rider. Long and lean. Cowboy tough. And that had been the problem. He was cowboy tough and cowboy stubborn.

The gelding took a couple sideways steps when she came to a stop and Shelby automatically adjusted the lead, bringing the horse back to where he was supposed to be, standing with his head at her shoulder. She brought her attention back to the man in front of her... the man who wasn't exactly bursting with explanations.

"Why are you here, Ty?"

"I'm back in Marietta for a while. I wanted to see you."

Direct. To the point. As Ty always was—when he talked about stuff. Good, because she was in no mood for polite games. She wanted him gone before her grandfather realized he was there.

"I see."

"We have unfinished business, Shelby."

The laugh burst out of her lips before she could stop it, startling the horse, who danced a few steps before stilling. "The business between us is long finished."

They hadn't kept in any kind of contact over the past four years, because she hadn't wanted contact. In her book, done was done and a clean break was the least painful. That was the theory anyway. But after experiencing a clean break, Shelby was pretty damned certain that she never wanted to go through a messy one.

Ty hadn't come back to Marietta once after leaving—not even for the rodeo. He'd called her exactly one time, shortly after taking off, turning her inside out yet again, and she'd told him no more calls. He hadn't attempted to contact her after that, which made her think he had understood they were through.

He shifted his weight again. His tell. "Four years is long time. I've never stopped thinking about you."

She stared at him for a moment. Was he honestly going here? Trying to pick things up again?

"Are you saying that you made the wrong choice four years ago?" When he'd chosen rodeo over staying and making a life with her?

"I made the only choice I could."

The only choice he could make was rodeo?

A spark of anger flickered to life. "But now that your career is over"—ended by a mare who'd gone down and crushed him more than half a year ago—"you're back?" She let out a snort. "I can't tell you how much I appreciate being your contingency plan."

"That isn't how it is."

"How else would you explain it, Ty?" Her tone had hardened, but she caught herself. "Never mind. You don't need to explain." Because needing an explanation meant she cared.

"Shelby…" He stepped closer and the gelding jerked his

head up.

Ty instantly stopped, giving the skittish animal time to figure out he wasn't an enemy and sure enough, the gelding lowered his head, stretched his nose out curiously. Ty knew horses.

He read them, which helped in his chosen line of work. "Maybe this isn't the time."

She forced a humorless smile and kept her voice even as she said, "You're right. This isn't the time. Nor is tomorrow. Nor the next day. I'll let you extrapolate from there."

If he'd just stopped by to say hello and warn her that he was back, she could have handled it just fine. Could have continued to believe she was through with the man. But to have the balls to insinuate that they weren't yet done?

Oh, she was *done*. Because she couldn't afford not to be.

The horse grew impatient, started dancing again, jerking Shelby's arm. It was her fault. She should have put him away instead of expecting him to stand patiently while two humans duked it out verbally.

The gelding swung his butt around, stamping his front feet, and Ty made a move, as if to calm the animal, but he stopped when she shot him a warning look. She'd handle things on her own. *Thank you very much.* Just as she'd done for close to forever. Besides, she didn't think she could stand it if he touched her. Didn't think she could handle the memories pouring back. As it was, it was killing her just being this close to him, fighting the unexpected emotions roaring through her.

She could tell herself she didn't care all she wanted—hell, she'd *convinced* herself she didn't care and had believed it… until he showed up. Now she cared. She cared about being hurt and being betrayed. She cared about Gramps being let down again. Her grandfather had loved Ty like a grandson and she was certain Ty's abandonment had hurt him as much as it'd hurt her.

"It was good seeing you, Ty." Lie of the century. "I'd appreciate it if you left before Gramps sees you. You hurt him, too, you know."

"I know."

That was when Shelby felt tears starting to burn her eyes. It didn't matter if they were angry tears, they were tears all the same and she would not cry. "I have work to do," she said abruptly. "You need to leave."

With that she turned and started leading the gelding toward the corral, escaping while she still had her composure. It wasn't the smoothest exit she'd ever made, but it would have to do. At least until she got a grip.

Her next horse, a paint mare she was evaluating as a prospect for a twelve-year-old beginning rider, was waiting for her, head hanging over the fence. The horse gave a gentle nicker, but Shelby barely registered the equine greeting.

She released the gelding and headed for the mare's pen, refusing to look back. Hell. Afraid to look back. Finally, after an eternity, she heard the truck door open and close. A moment later the diesel engine fired to life and relief surged through her, but it wasn't until the sound of the engine had faded into the distance that she allowed herself to turn and watch Ty's truck slow at the end of the long driveway, then ease out onto the county road. She turned her attention back to the paint mare, disgusted that her hands were shaking a little. Reaction. She'd wondered about this reunion for years—known it was inevitable, but hadn't expected it to affect her this badly.

The hell of it was, she knew this wasn't over.

Ty didn't give up easily and if he wanted to talk to her, he'd made another stab at it. But she wouldn't allow it to be here, with Gramps around... which meant she was going to have to take matters into her own hands and set a time and place for their final—and she meant *final*—showdown.

"Hey, Shelby." She turned to see Gramps standing on the porch.

He was still wearing his town clothes, which was good. It meant he was taking it easy today as he'd promised. He'd been moving more slowly lately and it bothered her. But the one thing her grandfather never did was admit to any kind of pain or weakness. A personal code of honor that drove her insane. He'd taken her in and cared for her in his own gruff way when her mom died, and now she was going to take care of him. The only problem was that he wasn't cooperating.

"Who was that?"

A lie? The truth? He was going to find out sooner or later, but later wouldn't kill him. And it would give her time to come up with strategy. "Somebody who needed directions."

"Ah. Looking for the River Road?"

Shelby just smiled rather than lie again and jerked her head toward the paint mare. "I'm going to be out on her for about an hour on the willow trail."

"Be careful."

She always was, which was why Ty wasn't getting a second crack at her.

AFTER LEAVING THE Forty-Six Ranch, Ty drove past what had once been Harding Farms and parked at the edge of the barley field, letting the engine idle as he studied his old home out the back window of his truck. His body ached, as if always did when he held in one position for too long, but this pain went beyond the dull throb of knitting bones and muscles. He felt as if every part of his body had seized up. Stress. Pure and simple.

He'd had no idea how to approach Shelby, but had figured since Carol Bingley, town gossip, had spotted him his first night in town, he be better off seeing her sooner than later. It probably wouldn't have mattered when he saw her— she was still as pissed at him as she'd been the day that he'd left. Which told him she cared enough to be pissed.

But it didn't give him a clue as how to proceed, so here he was, communing with his past, as if it would give him an insight into the future.

The farm had changed. The house was freshly painted and the barn had been reroofed—things his father hadn't been able to afford to do. Two little boys ran out of the house and made a beeline for the swings he and his brother, Austin, had played on years ago. The table he'd helped his father build was still there, too, covered with a red-checkered cloth. When his parents had sold out and moved, they'd left most everything behind, including the table he'd been so proud of. Granted, there wasn't a lot of room for a redwood picnic table on the postage stamp sized lawn in the Arizona snowbird trailer park his folks now called home. It was as if when his dad had given up farming, he'd wanted to deal with as little land as possible, so he and Ty's mom had headed south, where there were no Montana winters to contend with. No crops to worry about. No hunting or fishing either—at least not like there was in Montana, but Dad had been fine with that. Austin once said the land had wrung everything out of their father as he fought his losing battle to make the farm continue to pay for itself and support the small family that worked it. He'd given up his dream of being a champion bronc rider to take over the farm and had lost both—the dream and the farm. That was where Ty and Austin came in.

The woman came out of the house again carrying a large bowl. She paused on the steps, shading her eyes with her free hand as she stared in his direction. Ty put his truck in gear and pulled out onto the gravel road. He didn't want her to think he was casing the place when all he was doing was checking in on his past before moving forward with his future.

The forward part was still a little shaky. He wasn't done with his career, even though he'd truly believed he was when he'd announced his retirement after the wreck that had so thoroughly broken him early in the spring. About a week into recovery, he'd realized he had to give rodeo one more shot. Had to go out on his own terms, not on the terms of a cranky, white mare that had reared over backwards into the chute when the gate opened instead of charging out into the arena, thus doing Ty a world of hurt.

His therapist hadn't agreed and had told him it was time for a new career, a new life. But he loved his old one. The one that had taken him across the country time and again. Had battered his body and fed his brain. Had made him a winner, which helped compensate for his father's losses in life. His dad finally became a winner because his sons were winners—Ty in saddle bronc, Austin in the bull riding. Kenny Harding loved being the father of two champions... sometimes too much.

And at other times *way* too much.

Actually, his dad was a fucking *Dance Mom*, but Ty tolerated it because he understood his old man and loved him. It hadn't been easy for Kenny to accept that his eldest son's career was over, which was why Ty hadn't said one word about getting entry into the 78th Copper Mountain Rodeo. He wanted to test the waters, see if he still had what it took to continue his career, and he wanted to do it with as little fanfare as possible. He'd spoken to the head of the rodeo board and asked if they'd keep his entry quiet until day sheets were printed. Not a problem, they assured him, but they wanted to use his comeback ride for advertising next year if all went well. Ty had no problem with that. Maybe he'd be on his way to another championship by that time.

He took the left hand fork that led back to Marietta, past Copper Mountain, past the ghostly workings of the copper boom that had brought some of the first people into the area—his family included. When he pulled onto the highway to head south, he passed a flower-laden cross with a firefighter's coat hanging on it. Harry Monroe. He'd been a year ahead of Harry, a truly great guy, in school. Ty hadn't realized he'd been recently killed on the highway while helping a stalled out motorist until he'd eaten at the café and overheard talk of fund-raisers.

Life was short. Too short not to grab for all he could get. A championship. The woman he still loved... he wasn't waiting another four years to make things right with her. As it was, he felt damned lucky she was still single. She was strong and beautiful and, in some ways, scarred. She'd never fully gotten over losing her mother, and he probably hadn't helped matters by essentially abandoning her, but it was the only choice he could have made at the time.

He drove into Marietta and parked his truck next to the Graff, a beautifully refurbished Victorian hotel. He'd love to check in and stay for a couple of days, but he was hoarding money until after the rodeo, when he'd have a better idea as to where he was career-wise. He hadn't done a lot of planning when he'd left his friend's ranch in Texas to return home. Once he'd gotten entry into the rodeo, he'd pretty much climbed into his truck and started to drive, thinking if he got there a few weeks early, he could catch up with people, finish unfinished business, maybe find a place to bunk in exchange for some work—work that might become fulltime if the rodeo didn't go well. For the moment he was making do with a bedroll in the back of his truck and the public shower facility at the fairgrounds. He'd done worse.

An older woman he didn't know smiled at him as he got out of his truck and he touched the brim of his hat and smiled back. He started down the sidewalk to Grey's Saloon, figuring there was no better place to catch up on local goings on and see if anyone needed a day hand. He'd just passed the bank when a woman brushed by him from behind, moving with a limp that didn't slow her down much.

"Tanner. Hey."

Tanner McTavish turned and blinked at him before pushing her rust colored braid over her shoulder in a self-conscious gesture. "Ty. Hi." She smiled, but it didn't quite reach her eyes, possibly because Tanner was a friend of Shelby's. "I heard you were back."

Word traveled fast in Marietta, as always. He'd pulled into town yesterday evening and ate dinner at the café before parking his truck at the fairgrounds. The café had been almost empty, but Carole Bingley had been there with a friend, which explained everything. A compulsive gossip who worked at the pharmacy could spread a decent rumor with lightning speed.

"I am. I'm looking for a place to live for a while if you know of anything."

"Not off the top of my head." She cocked her head a little. "Does that mean you're staying?"

"For a while." An awkward silence hung between them before he asked, "Is Tucker going to be in town for the rodeo?"

Tanner's expression went stony at the mention of her sister's name. Apparently things weren't all that great between the twins. "She'll be here. I'll tell her you asked about her."

"No need." He and Tucker had gone out a time or two, but only as friends. She was flirty and fun, but she wasn't Shelby. "Just trying to catch up on who's where." He gestured toward the saloon. "Thought I'd start here."

Tanner gave a soft snort. "As long as you're not counting on Jason to fill you in, you should do fine."

The last thing Ty expected was that Jason Grey would fill him in on local gossip. The guy was grim, but he still ran the best establishment around—although Ty had yet to check out the new microbrewery, FlintWorks. He'd had some good times at the Wolf Den, further down the street, but he didn't think his body could take the trouble he sometimes got himself into there.

"I've got to run," Tanner said, adjusting her long purse strap on her shoulder. "Good seeing you."

"Good to see you, too." He walked on to Grey's and pushed through the door, stopping just inside so his eyes could adjust.

"The prodigal," Jason muttered as Ty approached the bar.

It was a dour announcement, but Ty had spent enough times in Grey's to know it was as close to an effusive greeting as he was ever going to get from the barkeep.

"One of many," he said.

Jason gave him a thoughtful look. "Yeah. Guess so." He poured a draft without asking and passed it across the bar. "Back for good?"

Again, very effusive for Jason, but Ty chalked it up to the fact the establishment was practically empty and no one would see Jason having an actual conversation.

"Depends on a few things."

Jason nodded, then headed to the other end of the bar where he started unloading a tray of glassware.

Conversation over. His plan of catching up with the locals was shot all to hell by the fact that there were no locals there to talk to. He didn't know the people sitting at the table in the far corner of the room, didn't know if they were new to the area or passing through. He'd only been gone for four years, but Marietta had changed. It seemed busier and not only because the rodeo weekend was approaching. He'd noticed new businesses and new houses. But the beauty of Marietta was that it was too far away from Bozeman to become a bedroom community, so the people there were people invested in the community.

Ty sipped his beer, then took his life in his hands and sauntered down the bar.

When Jason raised his eyes to glare, Ty said, "I'm looking for temporary work and a place to stay." He had some money tucked away, but hated to touch his emergency fund, which wasn't exactly huge.

"I'll keep my ears open."

Meaning nothing sprang to mind.

"Thanks." Ty gave a nod and made his way back to his stool, leaving Jason in peace. He finished his beer, pulled out his wallet and left some bills on the bar.

"Hey."

Ty turned at the door, surprised that Jason had spoken to him.

"Try Callen. For a place to stay. Heard she needs another cowboy on the Circle C. A guy just quit."

"Thanks." Ty gave Jason a quick nod, then stepped out into the bright Montana sun. First he'd find a place to stay, then he'd plot out his next move with Shelby.

Chapter Two

"WHEN WERE YOU going to tell me that Ty was back?"

Shelby looked over her shoulder at her grandfather, who'd just come around the barn, then turned her attention back to the mare she was unsaddling. "I didn't tell you because I needed some time to process. How'd you find out?"

"I had to phone in a prescription refill."

Carole Bingley. Of course. "I don't know why that woman still has a job," Shelby muttered as she pulled the latigo strap free of the cinch ring.

"That was him here this morning, wasn't it?"

"It was," Shelby agreed.

She pulled the saddle off the mare and Gramps automatically stepped forward to take it from her. After returning from the tack shed, he took a brush out of the bucket and started brushing the opposite of the horse from where Shelby was currying away sweat and grime.

"Looks like you gave her a workout."

"She gave herself a workout."

"Read your mood."

"She did indeed." Usually Shelby was able to put matters aside when she rode, lose herself as she communicated with the horse through her legs, seat, and hands. But not today.

Seeing Ty again had been almost surreal. She'd tried not to think about him over the years. Had done her damnedest to shove him out of her head, and she'd thought she had... until he'd driven to the ranch that morning. The impact of seeing him had made her want to curl up into a little ball somewhere dark and quiet and recover—which pissed her off to no end. That wasn't how she did things. She rebounded. She didn't curl up and feel sorry for herself.

"So how is he?" Gramps asked.

"He was moving slow."

"No surprise there."

None at all. Shelby hadn't given in to the temptation of finding Ty's career-ending wreck on YouTube, but Gramps had, and he'd described it in detail to her, even though she didn't want to hear those details. The horse had reared over backwards after the gate opened, pinning Ty against the chute, busting up his pelvis, shoulder and femur. If he were younger, he might have come back, but he wasn't younger and he'd announced his retirement after getting out of the hospital.

"Did he say why he was back in Marietta?" Gramps asked.

Shelby shot a look at him over the back of the horse, but he was bending low, brushing down one leg. This was shaky ground. Break her heart, fine. But she was not going to have Gramps get caught in the crossfire again.

"He didn't." He also hadn't said how long he'd be there.

"Well," Gramps said as he straightened up again. "I have a lot of prescriptions to refill, so I should have no trouble finding out what he's up to and whether or not he's staying for good."

Shelby brought her forearms up to rest on the mare's broad back. "Why do you care?"

"Because you do."

She opened her mouth to say she did not, but that was more of a lie than she could force out. "I do care, but only because I don't want people getting hurt again."

"People?" Gramps frowned at her. "You don't mean me, in addition to you?"

She shrugged. "You were no happier than I was when Ty took off."

"Different reason."

Shelby wanted to ask about the reason, but she also wanted to drop the conversation because if her stomach got any tighter, she wasn't going to be able to eat for the rest of the day.

"Shelby." She looked up, met her grandfather's gaze, read his concern.

"I can handle things."

"I know."

Of course he knew. She'd proven it a time or two. She'd handled it when her mother had died way too young. She'd handled all the usual teenage heartaches with only her friend, Cassie, and her team roping partner, Wyatt, for support. She'd handled Ty's abandonment.

"He told me he hadn't made a mistake in leaving me." Shelby didn't want Gramps to have any concerns about her taking up with Ty again. "Was pretty damned adamant about it. And I will not be seconds, Gramps. I don't think it's right that he went off and lived the life he loved and now that he's hurt and can't continue with that life, he's back for the next best thing. Believe it or not, being number two on his priority list doesn't warm my heart."

Her grandfather said nothing as he continued to brush and Shelby hoped the conversation was now over. She gave the brush one last quick flip on the mare's neck, then set it in the grooming bucket before once again meeting his shrewd gaze, hoping he couldn't see, even though she was truly done with Ty, being near him again had been unsettling.

"I'd thought better of him," her grandfather finally muttered.

He shook his head as if done with the matter, but just to make certain the subject was dropped once and for all, Shelby said, "I heard back from the Barlows."

"The ritzy ranch people?"

Shelby couldn't help but smile, despite her mood. A

transplanted Texan had built a sweet little hobby ranch ten miles north of Marietta, only to be driven out by the Montana winters after two years. He'd left behind a lovely cedar, glass, and stone house, state-of-the-art fencing, and barns. Gramps had told Shelby the Texan would never get what he was asking for his "ritzy ranch," but the place had been snapped up in less than a week by Paul Barlow, a tech-boom millionaire anxious to get away from the Seattle rain.

"Yep. They're bringing the horse by next weekend. I guess he's a little wild." Anyway, that was the impression she'd gotten when the proud new owner had described him to her.

"How old is he?"

"Nine."

Gramps cocked an eyebrow at her. "Kind of old to rehab."

Shelby just shrugged and untied the paint mare. "I'll evaluate him."

"Wish Uriel was still here."

Uriel had left for an outfitting job that paid full benefits instead of bare bones health care that Gramps offered. He still stopped by from time to time when Shelby or Gramps needed a hand with haying, but his new job kept him busy most days of the week during tourist and hunting seasons. Shelby understood why Uriel had taken the new job, but she'd been sad to see him go—not only had his departure added to her grandfather's workload, Uriel was now no longer there to help handle the tougher horses when necessary. Shelby was good, but she was also only five-foot-four and there were times when she needed muscle and height. Uriel had both.

Shelby made a wry face at her grandfather. "If the horse is more than I can handle, I'll send him back. You know I will."

Shelby wasn't one to give up, but there were times when common sense outweighed stubbornness and determination. She couldn't afford to get hurt, or to have her grandfather hurt.

"Was she your last ride for the day?" Gramps asked as Shelby released the mare and then returned for the grooming bucket.

"Yeah. I'm roping tonight."

"In town?"

She shook her head. "Wyatt's arena. The rodeo grounds tomorrow." Practicing for her big comeback at the Copper Mountain Rodeo with her long time team roping partner.

Funny how having Ty in the area put the prospect of roping in public—which had been unnerving the hell out of her for the past several weeks—into perspective. On a standard stress scale, Ty's return was a ten. Maybe an eleven. Competing in the rodeo without screwing up was now only a five or six.

Her grandfather reached out to take the grooming bucket from her as they started toward the barn. "Just focus on your roping and your horses and forget that Ty's anywhere in the vicinity."

Shelby gave a small snort. Excellent advice, but easier said than done... especially when she was certain he was going to seek her out again and would continue to do so until he considered the matter between them settled.

"YOU'RE A DAY too late," Callen Carrigan McAllister said, shaking her head. "We would have hired you, too."

"Then I guess it wasn't meant to be." Although he wished it had. It would have been a good solution all the way around—Callen would get help the temporary help she needed on the ranch and he'd get a place to live.

Callen smiled a little. "I'll let you know if I hear of anyone who needs a hand for a couple of weeks." She cocked her head. "Where are you staying?"

"I'm parked at the rodeo grounds. Sleeping in my bedroll in the back of the truck."

"Just like old times?"

When he'd first starting following the circuit he had spent a lot of time sleeping in the bed of his truck, driving insane distances, riding, then getting back into his truck to drive another insane distance. "Exactly like old times."

"You know... I may not be able to offer a paycheck, but I might have something more comfortable in the way of living arrangements. Hawksley's old camp trailer is still parked behind the barn. It's in rough shape, but I'd lend it to you. Indefinitely. I'll even give you a place to park it."

"I don't want to get in your way."

"You could park it in the aspen grove just past the cattle guard. Close to the county road, but you'd have your privacy. And if you find a place closer to town or on another ranch, cool."

Ty grinned. He wasn't one for charity, but Callen's no nonsense attitude made it easier. "I'll pay you rent."

"If it makes you feel better."

"It does."

"It just so happens that my husband is an accountant. I'll ask him what rent I should charge for a fifty-year-old camp trailer that may or may not have mice and get back to you."

"Thanks, Callen. Maybe we can shoot a game of pool sometime."

She grinned. "Yeah. We can wager on whether or not you pay rent."

"I HEARD THAT Ty's back." Wyatt Marshall shot Shelby a quick look before tightening his cinch and dropping the stirrup back into place.

Wyatt was her friend, but Shelby was getting pretty damned sick of hearing those words, as well as reading them on her phone screen.

She leveled a dark look at her long-time team roping

partner. "Your point?"

Wyatt shrugged and mounted his zillion dollar horse. "No point."

Shelby snorted. She was riding another of his zillion dollar horses—Ginger—who was so damned good at what he did that, when she roped, she only had to worry about herself, and what went on in her head—no easy task, since psyching herself out was what had gotten her in trouble back in the day. Twice she'd ruined their chances of being high school national champions by totally blowing her catches and thus pissing off a lot of Wyatt's friends and supporters. Wyatt had shaken off the losses and gone on to win the NFR. Shelby had given up roping. Retired a loser and told herself she didn't care if she ever touched a rope or rode into an arena again, so when Wyatt had asked her to partner with him a few months ago, she'd told him he was nuts. He persisted and she'd finally agreed. Only twice in her life had she walked away from a situation that had gotten the better of her—one was team roping and the other was her relationship with Ty. Roping she'd try again. All she was risking there was public humiliation.

"I need to break in this rope." She shook out the stiff loops as they rode toward the box.

A trailer pulled into the drive as they moved into position and she could see the dust trail of another truck and trailer approaching in the distance. Pretty soon the driveway would be packed with trailers, which was why she'd arrived early. She wanted to get her practice in and head home.

Wyatt's sister, Katie, was manning the chutes. She waited until Shelby was in position before asking, "Ready?"

"As I'll ever be," Shelby said.

"Hey, I heard that Ty's back," Katie added as she nudged the steer's head so that he was looking straight ahead.

Shelby let out a pained breath and Katie frowned quizzically at her before she released the animal. Wyatt and Shelby charged after the steer, which cut to the left instead of continuing along the rail. Wyatt missed his first catch and muttered a filthy word. Shelby laughed. It didn't happen often, but it felt good to know that Wyatt had bad days, too.

She roped three more times before calling it a night and starting home. Katie or Wyatt must have said something to the other ropers, because no one else helpfully informed her that Ty was back in Marietta—but she'd had the feeling all eyes were on her. And they'd be on her again when she and Ty inevitably bumped into each other in Marietta. Unless she hid out on the ranch until he left town.

You don't do chicken shit stuff like that.

Right.

But she wished she knew how long Ty planned to stay. She should have asked, but hadn't been thinking all that straight when they'd talked. She hadn't been thinking all that straight *after* they'd talked, which worried her. Why did he still have this kind of an effect on her? And what could she do about it?

Waiting for him to leave wasn't the answer, even if she allowed herself to do such a thing. If he'd come back to the area after retiring, it probably meant he planned to stay. Which meant she would see him. A lot. Marietta was a small town. Too small to effectively dodge an ex-lover.

Shelby slowed her truck to let a couple of white-tail deer cross in front of her, tapping her fingers on the steering wheel. She'd been debating strategy all day long, talking herself in and out of various approaches to the situation with Ty, but regardless of what she tried to talk herself into, there seemed to be only one effective course of action—to confront matters head on. To take charge rather than waiting for something to happen.

Hiding out wasn't going to give her any peace. If anything, it would make the ghosts of the past loom larger. Shelby didn't need large ghosts hulking about. She wanted to get on with her life.

Besides, she was embarrassed by almost breaking down in front of him. That gave him a slight advantage.

So you take charge.

Shelby eased the truck forward after the last deer had cleared the fence and disappeared into the field on the opposite side, frowning to herself as a strategy took form.

Take charge. Go on the offensive. That was the last thing Ty would expect.

Tell him how things are going to be.

So what if the mere idea had made her palms sweat on

the steering wheel? If she couldn't do this, then it meant Ty still mattered in ways she couldn't, and wouldn't, accept.

She started to smile as she rounded the last corner before home.

She had her strategy.

Chapter Three

"YOU'RE CERTAIN THE best defense is a good offense?" Cassie Johnson, Shelby's best friend, leaned closer as she spoke, looking as if Shelby had just suggested she'd like to jump off a bridge. They shared a small table at Flint-Works, which was getting crowded and a touch loud, despite the lovely open layout of the old train depot turned microbrewery.

"I know Ty and I'll be dealing with him regardless. I may as well set the time and place."

"High noon. Main street?"

That was what it felt like.

Cassie took a sip of her drink, then nodded at Shelby's untouched glass. "Maybe you do need to talk to him, so that you can get on with your life. I've never seen wine sit in front of you for so long."

Shelby raised the glass and took a healthy swallow, but she didn't much enjoy the excellent cabernet that ran down her throat. Stupid nerves.

"Better," Cassie said. "So you're going to hunt him down

and tell him how it's going to be?"

"As soon as I figure out how to get hold of him." Since her plan was only about twelve hours old, she hadn't done any ground work. Instead she'd waited for her bar date with Cass to bounce the idea off her friend, formulate a strategy and then put it into action. "I heard a rumor that he's staying at the Circle C." She'd also heard he was looking for work. The grocery clerk had been a veritable well of helpful information earlier that day after she'd announced to Shelby that Ty was back in town. "Since Saturday is my half day, I figured I'd drive out to see him tomorrow."

"Or you could stroll across the bar right now."

Shelby's heart jumped at her friend's calm statement. Despite her resolve not to react to anything Ty-related, Shelby's stomach tightened as she turned to follow Cassie's gaze to the entryway, where her ex-everything stood surveying the place. He was wearing his hat, of course, a blue plaid shirt, and worn jeans that weren't in any way tight, but somehow hinted at the hard muscles beneath the denim. Dark hair. Blue eyes. Crazy hot mouth. Oh, yeah. That was Ty.

He was so damned attractive that it hurt a little to look at him. He'd been hers, but he hadn't. He hadn't wanted another woman, but he'd wanted that damned rodeo and those damned silver buckles.

Well, he could have them and she hoped, in a very cliché way, they kept him warm at night. In fact, she wished they were keeping him warm at this very moment and that he wasn't here, because she wasn't yet ready to put her plan into action.

She turned back around, took another chug of wine, and got real with herself. If four years hadn't made her feel ready, what good would another day do?

No good at all.

Shelby pushed her chair back. The amazing thing was she'd worn a dress tonight. And makeup. She might not be mentally prepared, but physically she was ready.

"Now?" Cassie asked in surprise.

"Now." While they were in a public place, where it was so much easier to end a conversation. Besides, the quicker she acted, the more likely she was to hold the advantage. Ty wasn't expecting her to approach him.

Cassie raised her glass in a tiny salute, then shook her long blond hair back over her shoulders. "I'll be here when you're finished."

"Shouldn't take long."

She hoped.

TY SAW SHELBY the instant she got to her feet. And she saw him.

She left her friend at the table and started navigating across the room toward him, weaving in and around people. She approached a narrow space between two guys and flashed a smile at them before slipping through, making Ty feel as if he'd been hit in the gut. It'd been too long since he'd seen her smile, and from the way her face once again settled into a coolly detached expression when she looked back at him, he didn't think he'd be seeing it any time soon.

A guy standing at the bar reached out to touch her arm when she passed and Shelby stopped, pushed her long honey-brown hair back over her shoulder. It rippled down her back as she said a few words to him, then she nodded and once again zeroed in on Ty. He did her a favor and closed the distance between them before she'd taken too many more steps or been stopped by another guy.

As she came to a stop a few feet away from him, she smiled—for the benefit of the crowd, no doubt—because there was nothing close to a friendly expression in her eyes.

"Ty. I thought we might have a word." She motioned toward a lone bar stool at the opposite end of the bar and, when he nodded his agreement, she turned and started moving.

Ty followed, nodding at a couple of people on the way. Old acquaintances that appeared surprised to see him there with Shelby. He didn't slow down to talk, but instead kept his eyes on Shelby, letting his gaze slide down to the movement of her hips beneath the slick white fabric of the dress she wore, then bringing them back up to her face when she turned toward him before pulling out the barstool with one hand. Ty would have helped, but that would have meant getting close and instinct told him to keep his distance—at least until he knew what was going on.

The bartender, who was wearing the same overly bright blue shirt as the rest of the staff, with FlintWorks emblazoned across the front, took a quick sideways step to where Shelby had settled on the bar stool.

She smiled at him and nodded at her half-full glass of wine. "I'm good."

The guy gave Ty an expectant look as he leaned on the bar next to Shelby. "I'll have"—Ty frowned as he looked at the unfamiliar names on the tap handles—"your most popular draft."

"Triple C coming up."

Shelby's skirt had slid a little further up her smooth thigh now that she was seated and Ty tried to remember when he'd last seen her in a dress. A wedding maybe? She cleared her throat and he brought his gaze back up to her face.

She took a cool sip of wine. "First of all, I apologize for overreacting when you came to the ranch. You surprised me."

"Yeah. I kind of figured that. If I'd had your cell number, I would have called." He gave her a humorless half-smile. "And then we never would have seen each other in person."

"Probably not." She set the glass down, but kept her hand on the stem. "Like I told you before, over is over."

Ty let that one pass. If over was truly over, she wouldn't

have bothered to seek him out.

"I heard that you've found a place to live."

"Kind of." The bartender placed a perfectly poured mug in front of him, smiled, and moved on. They smiled a lot in this place. Whoever had trained the staff, had done a job of it.

"And that you're looking for work."

"I am." Ty took a drink, then gave an appreciative nod. Triple C was a decent brew.

"So you're staying." When he lifted his eyebrows at her blunt statement, Shelby have a small shrug. "You have no job, no family, no real place to live. You *could* have no job and no place to live pretty much anywhere. So why come back here?"

Her expression told him why he'd better *not* have come back.

Tough, Shelby. He'd played the game by her rules for four long years. Now he wanted to make some rules, set some parameters.

"I've got a couple of reasons."

She tilted her head and her hair slid over her shoulder. Ty wanted very much to push it back into place, to feel the silky strands move through his fingers. And if he did that, she'd probably deck him.

"A couple of reasons?" The politely conversational tone was at odds with the hard look in her eyes.

"For one thing, this is my hometown. It's the place I

want to be."

"In all your travels you never found another place?" She took a small sip of wine.

"Marietta has everything I want."

She gave him a long look. "You know you don't always get what you want, Ty."

He smiled a little. "True, but a lot of times I do."

Her hand tightened around the stem of the glass, but her gaze remained steady. "I better not be one of the reasons you came back." She took another a slow sip, studying him over the top of the glass.

"And if you are?"

The wine came down fast. "Don't waste your time, Ty. It won't be good for either of us."

"Maybe I've changed."

"So have I, Ty. I no longer need you."

"I don't know that you ever needed me."

She studied him for a moment, taking her time before answering. "Meaning that if I had, I would have come with you?" Her eyebrows lifted. "That goes two ways, Ty. You didn't need me, either."

That was where she was wrong. He *had* needed her, but he hadn't been ready to settle down. Making things permanent at the ripe old age of twenty-four wouldn't have worked, but he'd been a hair's breadth away from doing just that, for her—until his dad had talked to him.

"We aren't going to change the past."

She smiled grimly. "Or build a future."

"But maybe we can make a truce."

She considered for a moment, studying her wine again with a slight frown. A guy moved up to the bar next to her, squeezing into too small of a space, causing Shelby to lean toward Ty, whose first instinct was to tell the guy to back off.

"Excuse me," Shelby said to the oblivious asshole.

"Sorry," the guy muttered without looking at her or giving up an inch of space. Ty took a step forward, but Shelby sent him a warning look. *Not your fight.*

His mouth tightened, but he stayed where he was as the bartender approached. "Hey, Wade," he said. "Give the lady some room."

Wade let out a loud sigh and grudgingly stepped back so the Shelby no longer had to lean to the side. Moments later he had his beer and lumbered off without another word.

"See," Ty said. "Changed man. I didn't do one thing to adjust his attitude."

Shelby frowned at him. "Somehow I don't think so. I think you just pick your fights better." She looked across the room at the table where she'd been sitting when he came into the bar. Cassie Johnson sat there and she raised her chin in a little gesture of support. He was the enemy.

"You don't need back up," he said when Shelby turned her attention back to him.

Color crept into her smooth cheeks, but she didn't deny

that she'd been seeking moral support from her friend. He shifted his weight, turning his profile to her before looking at her again. "I understand that I hurt you, but things couldn't have played out any other way back then."

"Bull."

"Okay. Maybe I could have stayed here... but maybe you could have come with me." Shelby started slowly shaking her head and he allowed himself a faint smile, because the point was irrefutable. "You did what you had to do and I did what I had to do. It didn't mean we didn't care for one another."

"Just not enough, right?"

He moved a half step closer as a group of people squeezed into the area behind him and a guy accidentally elbowed him. "Maybe I cared too much to screw up your life while I dealt with the issues in mine." Shelby's chin rose, but he continued before she could speak. "Maybe I did what was best for both of us."

"Or maybe what was best for you."

"And maybe that was four *fucking* years ago and we've both changed." He leaned even closer then, so that the guy jostling him from behind wouldn't get every word. He would have asked her to leave the bar to talk in the parking lot, but had a very strong feeling that she wouldn't go. She wanted the crowd. "I was too young to settle down. I had things to do. Stuff to prove. Yes, I could have stayed, but we wouldn't have made it." And it was so damned hard to get those words out. Ty did not, as a rule, talk about the things that ate at him.

"So the end result is the same, Ty. We're not together."

She spoke coolly, but Ty read the tension in her expression. She was pissed as hell at him, but she was not indifferent. And that was a good thing, because indifference would have killed him. Anger he could deal with.

"So you're telling me that all hope is dead."

"You killed it when you left."

The guy behind Ty bumped into him yet again, this time almost pushing him into Shelby's lap. She jerked her upper body back, her breath catching as Ty regained his balance and took his hand off her thigh.

"Are you sure it's dead?" Because she was most definitely reacting to him.

She gave him a delicate sneer. "You have an ego, Ty. I'll give you that. I wanted to talk with you tonight to set things straight, and I wanted people to see me do it, so they will stop telling me you're back in town." She slid off the barstool and raised her chin so that she could hold his gaze. "For the record, we are *not* getting back together, and if that *hadn't* been your intentions, then I misread the situation and I apologize."

"You didn't misread." Not one bit. "And you've made your feelings on the matter damned clear."

"I'm glad we understand each other."

"We don't." He stated the simple truth.

Jostling guy hit him again and Ty gave him a quick elbow without breaking his gaze with Shelby and the man gave a low grunt. A guy could only take so much.

"Ty... I don't want to feel uncomfortable in my own town. If we see each other, we'll be civil. Right?"

"Pretend friends."

Her jaw muscles tightened. "If that's what you want. Eventually it'll feel more... normal... when we run into one another."

Dream on.

Ty didn't dare say the words out loud. "Then I guess I'll see you around."

She gave him a tight smile before edging her way by him. "Yes. I guess you will."

ONLY ONE LIGHT was on in her house when Shelby arrived home much earlier than anticipated. After talking with Ty, she figured she had two choices—stay out, get drunk, and go home with Cassie, or man up and deal with her maddening conversation stone cold sober. Drunk was tempting, but she'd be dealing regardless, so why start with a headache and cotton mouth the next morning?

Shelby let herself into the house as quietly as possible, on the off chance that Gramps was sleeping in his chair. He wasn't. She hung her keys on the hook near the door and slipped out of her shoes.

Gramps was a bona fide night owl. She couldn't remember the last time he'd been in bed before eleven and wondered if it was cause of concern. He had looked tired when he'd come into the house just before she left, but there was that flu bug going around... or maybe age was finally catching up with him. It happened—even to seemingly ageless guys like Les O'Connor.

There was no light coming out from under her grandfather's door when she crept down the hall to the bathroom. She would have loved to have unwound in front of the television, watched something mindless, but she decided to go to bed and not sleep instead.

Crazy how she felt as if she had to unwind after drinks, but that was *exactly* how she felt. On edge. Nerves taut.

Damn Ty Harding.

And damn her fool hormones.

Mine, mine, mine. They'd shouted every time he'd gotten close.

Not yours anymore, ladies, because we're not going to put ourselves through that *again.* It hurt like hell to want someone from the depths of her being and have them simply walk away. Yes, he was back, but Shelby wasn't about to settle for being the consolation prize. Ty's career was over and now he needed a home, a job. A pair of loving arms...

Her lips curled as she cranked on the water.

Not my arms, bud. She'd meant every word she'd said tonight... except that part about being friends. She didn't think she could do that, even for the sake of peace and harmony, but she'd said she'd try to fake it and she would.

Shelby scrubbed off her makeup and pushed her hair back from her face with wet hands. Life had been so simple until Ty drove back onto the ranch. So very simple.

If he was going to stay in Marietta, she was going to have to get used to seeing him. Get over this feeling that he was invading her turf—even if it was her turf because when he'd left, he'd essentially forfeited it to her.

He knows that. He's trying to fix it.

Shelby didn't want things fixed. She wanted back the life she'd had three days ago—a Ty-free life.

THE NEXT MORNING, Gramps beat Shelby out of bed, which wasn't unusual despite the fact that she usually went to bed before him. What was out unusual was the stiff way in which he moved across the kitchen, coffee cup in hand. He set the cup on the old Formica table and eased himself down into the chair, grimacing a little as he settled. His expression froze when he saw Shelby in the doorway frowning at him.

"Did you strain something?" Shelby asked as she headed for the coffee pot. She was careful not to look at her grandfather as she spoke. The more casual she kept the conversation, the less concerned she seemed, the more likely she was to get the truth. Or something approaching the truth. Her grandfather was pretty stoic.

"Woke up feeling a little stiff." He allowed, curling a hand around his coffee cup.

"Sleep wrong?" Shelby crossed the kitchen and sat in the chair across from him. She didn't dare sip the steaming hot coffee she set down in front of her.

"That's probably it."

"I'm sure that explains the bruise on your arm, too," she said mildly.

Gramps's gaze dropped to his left forearm where a bruise was indeed blooming near his elbow. "Huh. Didn't notice that."

Shelby took a chance on the coffee and burned her tongue. She set the cup down and wished for the zillionth time that her grandfather liked drip coffee instead of the boiled cowboy coffee he'd grown up drinking. But if he was making the coffee, she was keeping her complaints to herself.

"What did you do?"

He gave a small shrug. "Want some eggs?"

"Wouldn't mind."

He started to push himself up out of his chair then stopped when the pain hit him.

So much for trying to fake out your granddaughter.

"Sit down. I don't mind cooking." She had to wait for her coffee to cool anyway. She got out of her chair and headed for the fridge. "You were about to tell me what happened to you."

Gramps let out a breath. "Old age, near as I can figure."

Shelby took out a carton of eggs. "Just snuck up on you? Bruised your elbow and hurt your leg?"

"Hip."

"What happened to your hip?" She pulled a bowl out from the cupboard.

"I overdid it fencing."

Shelby turned, the bowl still in her hand. "Fencing? What fence?" All of their fences were in good shape unless a cow had recently gone through one.

Gramps pressed his lips together. "The fence along the creek on the grazing lease."

"There is no fence along the creek." Unless the people who'd recently purchased the land her grandfather leased to feed his cattle had built one. As far as she knew, that hadn't happened.

"There will be. The new owners changed the terms of the agreement and I have to fence off the riparian, except for two watering areas. They want it done before the snow flies, so it's ready come spring, when we turn out."

"When were you going to tell me about this new deal?" Because Gramps had renewed the lease for the adjoining property over two weeks ago and had never said one word about new fencing.

"You have a full plate."

Shelby turned back to the bowl and started cracking eggs into it. She did have a full schedule. She worked horses for eight hours a day, five-and-a-half days a week. Sunday was for catching up on hours she'd had to use for other things—doctors, dentists, grocery shopping. Roping practice... she'd give that up, except that Wyatt was counting on her to do her part in the Copper Mountain Rodeo. That was part of being a team roper—one counted on their partner.

Gramps got out of his chair and crossed the room, moving better than he'd been before he knew that Shelby was watching, and she had a feeling it was costing him.

"I've been working on this fence for two days now, using the posts in the stockpile and getting an idea of how much more materials I need to buy." He raised a hand when Shelby shot him a look. "It's still my property, kiddo, and if I want to fence it without help, so be it."

"I can see that's working out really well for you." She started stirring the eggs a little harder than necessary. The creek went on forever through the lease, winding instead of cutting straight across. "You can't do that much fencing alone. You need a crew."

"I could barely afford Uriel. Hell. I couldn't afford Uriel. Not year around anyway. He expected more money than Ty." Because Ty had only worked for them part-time before he took off to pursue his rodeo dreams.

"We need to get someone. I'd help if I didn't have a full schedule."

"Maybe I can put a notice up at the feed store."

"Or maybe Ty could have his old job back." The idea came out of nowhere.

Crazy, yet somehow sane, and Shelby felt oddly calm as she spoke. What better way to prove they were well and truly over? To take command of the situation? This would be the ultimate in command... she'd be his boss.

When she chanced a glance at her grandfather he was literally gaping at her.

He snapped his mouth shut, then said, "I thought..." His voice trailed off as if he was afraid of saying something wrong.

"Ty and I talked last night. Things are truly over. You need the help." And Ty owed Gramps for taking off like he did.

If he was back in Marietta, he might as well pay his debt. He knew Gramps. He knew the ranch.

"Maybe one of the fire crew."

"Or maybe someone who you can work with." Because her grandfather was not an easy boss. "Can you afford to pay Ty his old wage for a few weeks?"

Shelby's business was separate from the ranch, which was solely owned by her grandfather. She paid rent on the corrals and the tack sheds at her insistence, hoping it helped Gramps make ends meet during the lean times. It seemed to be working. He hadn't shipped cows to pay unexpected bills in a long time, but he hadn't paid anyone a salary since Uriel left.

"I can afford part-time help."

Shelby put butter in the pan heating on the stove and slowly swirled it. "Good. I'll see Ty today."

"I don't know that I like this. Not after..." His voice

trailed yet again and Shelby gave him a bland look over her shoulder.

"I can handle it."

IT WASN'T HARD to find Ty's small camp trailer, parked on the edge of the Carrigan property, not far from the cattle guard. He'd set up in an aspen grove and when she turned down the pasture track leading to his camp site, he came out from behind the trailer, bare-chested, his shirt in one hand. She hoped he would do them both a favor and put his shirt on. Soon. This mission was hard enough without the added distraction of trying not to look at his torso.

But this mission also felt right. If she spent time around Ty, the ghosts of the past would be laid to rest. It was very much like sacking out a green colt. By exposing the young horse to the things that triggered or frightened him in a slow and methodical way, eventually the colt accepted them as commonplace and no longer frightening. In this case, she was the colt.

She eased the truck around a water-filled rut, reiterating to herself that this was a good plan.

She and Ty might have their issues, but she trusted him to have Gramps's back if he hired on to do the job. To look out for her grandfather and keep him from overdoing things physically. Yes. Good plan.

Ty had his shirt on by the time she stopped her truck

and got out of it. It was buttoned crooked, but she could live with that. She just didn't want to see his chest, see the faint scar crossing his pecs that she used to trace with her index finger. And her tongue…

Stop.

Too late. The image filled her mind, made her insides tumble.

"Shelby." Ty's gaze was wary. "I can honestly say that this is a surprise."

"I imagine." She came around to the front of her truck, felt the heat on the engine on her back. "I'm here with a business proposition."

"Yeah?"

"Are you still looking for work?"

"I haven't nailed anything down yet."

"Would you consider short-term?" When he tilted his head, silently asking for details, she continued, "Gramps has to fence the riparian on the lease. It's too much for him to do alone."

"Uriel isn't there?"

"He's outfitting. Took the job last year. Gramps has been trying to do everything on his own."

"Can't find a replacement?"

"Gramps doesn't pay all that well."

Ty's eyes narrowed as he studied her. "You'll forgive me if I find it odd that you're here offering me a job after our discussion last night."

JEANNIE WATT

"I get that. But Gramps needs help, and you did kind of cut him off at the knees when you took off."

"So I owe him."

"Pretty much." Ty shifted his gaze down to his scuffed boots, one of which had a pant leg jammed into it, while the other pant leg fell down over the boot where it belonged. He'd gotten dressed in a hurry—probably when he heard her truck pull over the cattle guard. She glanced at the trailer, then an awful thought struck her. What if he wasn't alone?

It. Doesn't. Matter.

In fact, it would be a good thing. Problem solved. Right?

Shelby tore her eyes away from the trailer and met Ty's gaze once again. She shifted her weight. Despite the crisp early morning air, her thin cotton shirt was sticking to her back. "I trust you to keep an eye on Gramps. Not let him overdo it."

"Seems anyone could do that?"

"Gramps can't buffalo you or strong arm you. One less worry for me."

Ty kicked the dirt at his feet with the toe of his boot. "Can I move the trailer onto the ranch?"

Shelby's heart kicked. Ty. On the ranch. Several hours a day working with Gramps was one thing. His living there was another.

She almost said, "I don't think so." But she stopped herself. It was a reasonable request given the fact that the Carrigan Ranch was a bit of a drive from the Forty-Six and they weren't paying high wages. One corner of her mouth tightened. "That makes sense. Where'd you get the trailer?"

"Long story." She tilted her head. "Callen felt sorry for me."

"She's okay with you moving it?"

"Mine until I don't need it any more. When do you want me to start?"

"Does tomorrow work? Because Gramps is out there today busting his ass alone."

"Tomorrow it is. I'll talk to Callen and move the trailer later today."

"Thanks, Ty." She meant it.

"Shelby?"

She had her hand on the truck's door handle when he said her name.

She glanced back at him. "Yes?"

He sauntered a few steps closer, moving with only a hint of a limp from his wreck earlier that year, everything about him so damned... male. "Don't you want to lay down some ground rules?"

"I'm pretty sure you can figure out the ground rules. You're there to help Gramps."

"Then let me lay down mine."

Shelby's eyebrows lifted as she let go of the door handle. "You have ground rules?"

"You aren't the only one who can draw a line in the sand, Shelb. I did as you asked and stayed away for four long years. It wasn't easy."

"You're making me seriously rethink this job offer."

Ty simply raised an eyebrow, telling Shelby he was now aware that she needed him more than he needed her. He knew the ranch; he knew the operation… he knew Gramps.

She cleared her throat, but her voice was still a touch husky when she asked, "So, what are your ground rules?"

She expected him to move closer, to drive home his point that, in a way, *he* was now in the power position. He did not.

Instead he crossed his arms over his crookedly-buttoned shirt and said, "I can't change the decisions I made four years ago."

A long measure of silence followed. Shelby finally broke it. "What are your ground rules, Ty?"

"My ground *rule* is very simple. We start fresh. The past is gone. We let it go."

Shelby opened her mouth to protest, but he held up a hand and she closed it again.

"I didn't say you needed to like me or consider me a friend. I'm kind of getting a clear picture of your feelings there. But we let the past go. Clean slate."

"You're asking a lot." She folded her arms over her chest, mimicking his stance. "Because, believe it or not, I harbor some resentment."

"You hide it well."

Shelby's lips twitched.

"Do this and I'll make certain your grandfather feels like he's working his ass off when he's not."

Shelby blew out a breath. Then she gave a curt nod and dropped her arms. If it were anyone else she'd shake his hand, but it wasn't anyone else. It was Ty and just being close to him made her nerves dance in a crazy way.

"Deal," she said.

He smiled that cool half-smile of his. "I'll have the trailer moved by the end of the day."

Chapter Four

KEEPING AN OLD man from hurting himself was a lot of work… especially when the old man was a guy who didn't want anyone doing anything for him.

Finally, after Les had dug his fourth posthole, Ty reached out and took the diggers from him. Les's gloved hands fell to his sides as he shot Ty a fierce look.

"What are you paying me for?" Ty asked, holding the diggers out of reach.

"To help me fence." Les growled.

"Then stop paying me to *watch* you fence."

Les pulled in a breath that expanded his chest a good inch or so, and Ty fully expected an argument to follow, but instead Les's cheeks puffed out and then he exhaled.

"I don't know if I'm doing the right thing, letting you be here on the ranch."

"Why wouldn't it be the right thing?" Ty asked.

"Because I worry about Shelby."

Ty had known this talk was coming and was relieved Les had decided to dive in shortly after their workday had begun.

The sooner they had this settled, the sooner Les would stop trying to kill himself by working too hard.

"It ruined her when you took off." Les reached out and took the diggers from Ty. He walked to the next stake and stabbed them into the moist ground. Ty followed.

"It would have ruined her if I'd stayed. I needed to go."

"She tried to hide it from me, but the girl was hurting." Another stab. "Bad. It took her months to get back to her old self."

Ty tightened one corner of his mouth and looked past Les to the treelined horizon. "She's doing okay now. We agreed to put the past behind us."

"How so?" Les asked suspiciously.

"We're going to… start fresh."

The old man snorted and put his back into the next stab of the diggers. "Well, I'd appreciate it if you didn't start at all." He sounded serious.

"If you thought that was a danger, then why did you agree to let me come back to work?"

"Shelby set this whole damned thing up."

"Kind of blindsided you?"

Les leaned on the diggers, perspiration gleaming on his forehead. Shelby was going to kill him if Les did himself harm on his watch. "Yeah. Pretty much."

"So why not kick me off the place?"

"Because I need the help," Les admitted gruffly.

"Not from what I've seen."

"I'm working out some frustrations, okay? I can't control Shelby's life, but I worry about her. Having you back in Marietta... I figured maybe I could talk to you, get you to see that you and Shelby... well, it's not good for her" He met Ty's gaze then. "I like you, Ty. Always have. But I can't have Shelby getting hurt again."

"And if I do hurt her, are you going to cut off my nuts or something?"

The look Les gave him before giving the diggers another sharp jab into the ground was answer enough. Hurt Shelby and he'd be singing soprano.

"Gotcha."

"Like I said, I like you, Ty. You were kind of like a grandson to me." He grunted as the diggers went deep into the damp earth. "But if I have to choose, I choose Shelby."

SHELBY FINISHED HER last horse before Gramps and Ty got back to the ranch. If her grandfather had been working alone, she would have waited for him and been late to roping practice. But since Ty was working with him, she went into the house, washed her face, re-braided her hair and put on a clean shirt, ignoring her dusty jeans and boots. Peace of mind on some fronts, not so much on others.

Late last night, after Ty had finished setting up the trailer and disappeared inside, she'd given into temptation and searched for the video of his career-ending wreck on

YouTube. It wasn't hard to find, and watching Ty get smashed by the horse as she went over backwards into the chute made Shelby feel sick. He was so damned lucky to be alive, and, after losing her mom to cancer when she was ten, and her friend, Harry Monroe, to a senseless highway accident only weeks ago, the realizations hit hard.

But he was alive. He'd lived through the wreck, he was here, and now she needed to get used to having him around. Her body had yet to get the message that, even though he was close, he was now off-limits—that what had been hers to touch was hers no more.

Time and exposure would help. She may never feel totally comfortable being close to Ty, but she could feel easier about it. More... normal.

That was the plan, anyway.

Clamping her straw hat on her head, Shelby headed out to the truck, loving the fact she didn't have to bother with a trailer, since she always rode one of Wyatt's horses at practice. Her trusty roping horse, Dapples, was twenty-five years old and permanently on pasture. His speed was gone and his arena days over. Shelby had thought her arena days were over, too, until Wyatt had called. Practice was helping, but she still had reservations about roping again.

You are tough. You can do this. Besides, how often did one get to compete with a world champion cowboy? One she'd made mud pies with?

He hated it when she brought that up.

Wyatt was already warming up when she got there. Ginger was tied at the rail, his bridle hanging from the saddle horn. Shelby slipped the bit into his mouth and he lowered his head so she could put the bridle over his ears. Well-trained, as were all Wyatt's horses.

"Have you been practicing on the ground?" Wyatt asked as she rode into the arena to join him. He might be roping for fun, but he expected certain things from his partner.

"Some."

"Turn that 'some' into 'a lot' before the rodeo."

"Yes, sir." The ropers creed was to never stop roping. She'd been putting in an hour on the dummy three times a week, but she'd up that. When she'd been competing, she'd practiced on the ground before school and on horseback after. Her hands had been callused and unladylike, despite her gloves, but she hadn't cared because the guys she went out with also rodeoed and understood calluses.

Ty understood calluses. And he'd certainly known how to use his own callused hands to advantage...

Stop.

It turned out to be a good night practice-wise. She only missed once and even then managed to pick up one heel. A penalty, but still a score.

"You're quite the dead-eye," Wyatt said as they dismounted at the edge of the arena.

"I know. Crazy."

"Why crazy?" he asked mildly.

Shelby shot her friend a look and figured there was no sense lying about matters. "I thought I'd be more distracted. Ty's back."

"Yeah, I know," Wyatt said dryly. "We discussed that the last time we roped. Katie said you looked like you wanted to take her head off when she mentioned it at the chute."

Shelby settled a hand on the back of her saddle. "No. I mean *back*, as in back on the ranch."

Wyatt's dark eyebrows shot up. "Why in the hell is he back on the ranch?"

Shelby appreciated the protective note in his voice, but she didn't feel like defending herself to her roping partner. "Long story."

"Bore me."

For a moment their gazes clashed and finally Shelby gave in. "Gramps needs help. We have to fence the riparian and I have too many horse contracts to help him."

"So he's working for your grandpa."

"And living on the ranch in a camp trailer."

Wyatt narrowed his eyes at her in a *"really?"* expression.

"Hey," Shelby muttered, sounding only slightly less defensive than she felt, "I'm going to see him anyway in Marietta. It's only for a few weeks."

"Total immersion?"

Shelby blinked at him. She'd underestimated his understanding of the situation. "It seemed the best course of action. If I'm around him a lot, then it'll desensitize things.

Kind of like sacking out a green colt."

"If you say so."

Shelby shrugged as she pulled the reins over her borrowed horse's head. "To be frank, I have no idea what the best course of action is or was, but Gramps needed help. Ty knows him and he knows the ranch. Gramps won't be able to bully him or pull the boss card, both of which he'll do with someone else."

They started leading their horses to the gate, sandy dirt crunching beneath their boots, making it difficult to walk.

Finally, Wyatt said, "Well, having him there hasn't hurt your roping none." He gave her a sideways look. "Maybe because we both know that worry keeps you from psyching yourself out about roping."

"There's nothing to worry about."

"You sound like you're convincing yourself."

"More like reminding myself."

Wyatt gave her a long look and she could see he was on verge of saying something she didn't want to hear. "You really think this is a good idea, Shelby? Because I don't."

"Well, aren't you just a ray of sunshine?" She took her hat off and slapped it on her leg to shake off the arena dust, then put it back on her head.

"I'm a guy. And a realist."

"It will work, Wyatt. Because I'm going to make it work."

"More power to you, Shelby. And… good luck."

"Thanks." Although she would have felt better about Wyatt's well wishes if they hadn't been delivered on such a dark note.

TY IDLY RUBBED his bad shoulder as he walked back to the camp trailer. After the "talk", Les allowed Ty to take over the posthole diggers and they finished the fence braces in the tricky spots that Les couldn't access with the tractor and auger. The creek meandered through the leased land in long lazy turns and the plan was to fence the north side, then tackle the south. The north side was the more challenging of the two, since that was where the willows flourished. If they got too close to the creek, the posts had no purchase. If they got too far away, Les was losing feed.

He walked into the trailer, wondered what to do about dinner. Granola bars or a trip to town to eat at the café? He was beat, didn't feel like driving, but he was hungry. And pretty damned dirty. He'd gone knee deep in muck twice that day. Les had offered him use of the washing machine, but Ty hadn't given an answer. He was on the ranch, but he wasn't going to push things. He knew Shelby well enough to understand that even though she'd asked him onto the place, she had limits. And if he pushed, she was going to push back.

He had a narrow line to walk here.

His trailer was set up next to the old homestead house on the west side of the barn, where he could shower in a place larger than a postage stamp—no, the camp trailer's shower was actually smaller than that. Les used the building to store grain and excess tack and to doctor young animals. The shower had pretty good water pressure and, even though the air in the unheated bathroom was cold, the water was hot. *Thank you fifty-year-old gas water heater.* Ty stripped down, leaving his clothes on a beat-up old chair, then stepped under the spray, lifting his chin to let the water hit his upper chest and loosen the tight muscles there. If he felt this bad after digging holes, then riding was going to beat the shit out of him.

Wouldn't be the first time.

Hopefully wouldn't be the last.

Ty finally grabbed the soap when the water started to cool. By the time he'd lathered up and rinsed off he was dealing with frigid. He'd time things better tomorrow.

He shoved his damp skin into his clean jeans and shrugged into his shirt. He rarely missed a nightly session with his free weights, but today he'd done enough exercise; all he wanted was a beer and food. And maybe some heat ointment. Damn, but he was sore. Apparently therapy and weights hadn't prepared him for the reality of trying to outwork an old man.

Les had definitely challenged him, but as the day wore on, Ty had begun to see why Shelby was concerned about her grandfather. Les stopped what he was doing at least twice to grab hold of a post and stand stock still, as if waiting for a spell to pass. The second time Ty asked if he was dizzy.

Les had simply frowned at him and said, "Straightened up too fast."

Good answer, except he hadn't been bent over. And then there was the matter of him admitting he needed help. That never would have happened back in the day, which made Ty glad that Shelby had swallowed her pride and asked him to hire on. Les honestly did need help now, but once the fence was built, there wasn't much to be done on the place over the winter, except for feeding and catching up on the mechanic-ing. Les could handle that and, who knew, maybe come spring, if the circuit didn't go well—

What the fuck?

Since when did he think like that?

He'd thought that way for a few weeks after being broken to the point the doctors told him he probably wouldn't ride again. He'd announced he was through, but looking back, he half wondered if that had been to get his dad off his back... and maybe the concussion hadn't helped his cognitive abilities.

Well, he'd set speed records healing, had done all of his rehab, bought a new vest in case another horse decided to smash him in the chute. Broken or not, he was riding in the Copper Mountain. If he didn't destroy himself, then he was set to start the new rodeo season in October.

Chapter Five

S HELBY SET A crock of stew on the table and called her grandfather to dinner before heading to the cupboard for dinnerware. If it wasn't for the slow cooker, they'd be eating peanut butter and crackers most nights, because neither of them had time to cook during their jam-packed days.

Things would slow down as soon as the snow fell. She'd stop training full-time and start pinching pennies until training season started again. She was usually able to get on during the Christmas season at one of the larger stores in Livingston or Bozeman, even though Gramps hated her making the drive. Money was tight year around, but she was doing what she loved and living frugally seemed a reasonable trade off.

"Gramps," she called again.

Nothing.

She set down the bowls she'd just pulled out of the cupboard and peeked into the living room. Her grandfather was sound asleep in his chair, even though he and Ty had quit almost an hour earlier than they had the day before—

possibly because Gramps had wanted to be there when her new horse arrived—the one from the ritzy ranch people.

Fine. The stew would keep. And if she left for her evening out in Marietta before he woke up, she'd prop a note on the table telling him where she was.

Gramps began snoring as she finished her meal. Shelby did her best to find comfort in the sound, although part of her wondered why, three days into Ty's stint on the ranch, her grandfather was still coming home exhausted. Ty was supposed to be doing most of the work.

One way to find out was to ask.

She washed the bowl and put it into the drain rack to dry, then went to the kitchen window just in time to see Ty disappear into the machine shed.

Quarry sighted. She quietly let herself out the back door.

"Hey," she called when Ty came out of the shed again and started toward the barn, his limp slightly more pronounced than it had been when he first arrived. He stopped and turned and her heart jumped as their gazes connected. He was so damned gorgeous, all hard lines and muscle.

Shelby shoved the thought aside. Parts of her couldn't stop wanting him—the parts that didn't know any better. The rest of her was still damned angry and hurt and not about to slide down that slippery slope again.

"Hi," he said on a cautious note. It was the first words they'd exchanged in a day and a half.

"How's the fencing going?"

"Slow. Lots of muck to contend with."

"Are you letting Gramps do more than he should?"

He blew out a breath. "I'm doing my best to rein him in."

"I thought you said you could make him *think* he was busting his ass."

"In the old days I could have."

"What's changed?"

"I think that he's trying to get this fence done as soon as possible to get me off the ranch and away from you."

Shelby stared at him. "You're kidding."

Ty gave his head a slow shake.

"But he agreed to this plan."

"Probably because he knew it was senseless not to."

"Meaning…?"

"Once you get an idea in your head, you're like a terrier with a rat."

Shelby frowned at him. "I'll take that as a compliment."

"Take it as you will. I'm honestly trying to take the lead."

"Try harder."

"Will do."

Shelby glanced at the machine shed and saw that Ty had ripped into one of the four-wheelers. Her shoulders slumped. "Please don't tell me we're looking at something major?"

"Not certain, but it's running rough. Thought I'd take a look before showering."

Ty wiped his hands on a rag, slowly taking the grease off

each finger. "I haven't seen much of you since arriving."

She gave a small shrug as her pulse bumped again. "I have a full schedule. In fact, I have another horse arriving tonight."

"I heard."

Good. "I'm glad you and Gramps are talking. Sometimes he doesn't."

"I worked with the man for a couple of years."

"You also screwed with his granddaughter and he doesn't like that."

"No kidding." He gave his hands a final wipe. "Is that why you're avoiding me?"

"Avoiding you?"

"I've seen the neighbor more often than I've seen you."

"I have no need to avoid you. We're starting over, re-member? Clean slate?"

His mouth curved. That gorgeous, treacherous, could-do-things-to-her mouth. "I remember," he said softly.

The words flowed over her like a caress. This was not going well.

"Maybe I'll stop by after you get off work each day and touch base."

She meant the words to be sarcastic, but Ty took them at face value. "Good idea. I could tell you how far we've gotten. Give you a Les report, since he's the reason I'm here."

"Yes. Good idea." *Hoisted on her own petard.* But full immersion was the name of the game and she'd been side-stepping—to the point that Ty had called her on it.

"Cool."

"Cool." She echoed. "I need to take care of some stuff in the house. Like I said, I have a horse coming in about an hour and some business in town after that."

"Busy evening."

She gave a small shrug. "Keeps me out of trouble."

She hoped. Because trouble incarnate was standing a few yards away from her.

TY FIGURED OUT the problem with the fuel line shortly after Shelby marched away toward the house, patched things up, then headed to the homestead house to shower.

She wasn't avoiding him. Right. He'd worked on this ranch before and Shelby had been all over the place then. Now she tended to make a beeline from the horse corrals to the house as soon as she finished training and feeding. And if she was avoiding him, then she wasn't indifferent to him.

Ty showered quickly, cranking off the water before it started to go cold. Three days in and he was no longer sore in places he hadn't been sore in a while. He toweled off quickly, slipping into his jeans and beat up moccasins before slinging the towel over his bare shoulder. When he stepped out of the house, he shivered as the much-warmer early evening air hit him. It had to be twenty degrees colder in the house than it was outside. He'd just opened the trailer door when he heard the distinctive rattle of a horse trailer coming up the drive.

No doubt the horse that had Les concerned.

He and the old man were finally to a point where they were talking while they worked and Les wasn't happy about Shelby taking on the horse arriving that evening—the horse that was here now.

"Money and contacts are no reason to take on a nine-year-old rehab case," he'd muttered more than once that day as they'd starting stretching wire along the first section of completed posts and braces.

"He might just need a firm hand." Ty had offered. It wasn't unusual for inexperienced owners to let their horses take control.

"I heard about this horse. In the feed store." Les had shot him a dark look and shook his head.

"The matter just… came up?" Ty asked.

"No. I asked if anyone knew these Barlow people. Someone knew the horse. He's trouble."

All the more reason for Ty to be there when the beast was unloaded. He went inside and pulled on his shirt then slapped his hat over his damp hair.

A shiny, blue truck and matching trailer pulled to a stop near the corrals. Shelby was already halfway down the walk when Ty rounded the corner of the homestead house.

A man and a woman got out of their respective sides of the expensive truck. The guy looked like he was trying very hard to look working class. He had on a chambray shirt—

carefully pressed—and jeans, but that was where working class stopped and money began. His boots were lizard, his buckle sterling, his hat custom. Ty knew a lot of working guys with those same outfits, but this guy's stuff was all shiny new.

"Hello," the woman called to Ty as she got out of the rig. She pushed her very straight long, chestnut hair over her shoulder and started toward him. Her mile-long legs were encased in tastefully ripped and mended jeans, which were in turn tucked into thousand-dollar boots. Her shirt was simple red-plaid flannel, rolled at the sleeves, but her hat was a multi-x beaver.

Money, money, money.

Which was a good thing for Shelby—unless this horse was as bad as Les feared.

"Hi," he replied before gesturing toward Shelby. "Your trainer."

"Of course!" She and the guy both turned and shifted course toward Shelby.

The guy extended his hand. "Paul Barlow. My girlfriend, Blake." Who apparently didn't have a last name.

Handshakes were exchanged and then Shelby introduced Ty. More handshakes.

The trailer started rocking as the horse inside started pounding the floor with his front feet.

"He's nervous," Blake murmured as she glanced at the trailer, looking almost proud. "He's so beautiful. I can't wait to ride him with my friends."

Shelby smiled noncommittally.

"Do you want some help unloading him?" Ty asked her in a low voice.

The trailer continued to rock as the impatient animal did his number inside.

"Is he tied?" Shelby asked Paul.

"My man couldn't get the job done, so I had him leave him loose," Paul said.

My man?

"If you want to back the trailer to the gate, we'll just unload him straight into the pen. Stop about four feet away." Shelby looked expectantly at Paul, and the guy went a little pale before drawing himself up a little taller.

Blake laughed. "We're game, if you want to take a chance with your gate. We just bought this gooseneck." She smiled at Ty. "Maiden voyage."

Paul did not appear to enjoy Blake's candid comments, but Ty did. Funny how it was possible to really dislike a guy within seconds of meeting them. And from the way Paul was eyeing him, it appeared the feeling was mutual.

"I'll do it," Shelby said.

"I… uh…" Paul started to shake his head as if the thought of a woman behind the wheel was too much for him.

"Let her do it," Blake said to Paul with a come-on-now smile. "It's her gate."

Paul struggled with his manhood, then said, "The keys are in it."

Shelby got into the truck and put it in gear, pulling it around and then backing smoothly so the trailer was about four feet directly in front of the corral gate. She got out of the truck and walked to the trailer, nodding at Ty. He opened the gate until it met the back of the trailer on the driver's side and then Shelby opened the trailer door, forming a perfect alley to the pen. The coal black horse approached the edge of the trailer, snorting loudly before he launched himself out of the trailer and raced wildly into the pen.

"His name is Evarado." Blake said without taking her eyes off the horse, who was indeed a magnificent animal.

"Unusual," Shelby murmured as she swung the gate closed.

Ty handled the door to the trailer.

"It's Spanish for brave." Blake rested a hand on the rail, watching as the horse paced the fence, tossing his head and looking for a way out. He gave a shrill whiny, which several horses answered. He'd have every equine on the place stirred up in short order.

Blake sighed. "Isn't he a beauty?"

"Just lovely," Ty said dryly as the horse snorted and stamped again.

"You said you'd have him for thirty days," Paul said to Shelby.

"I'll evaluate him for a few days and let you know."

"I don't want him back until he's tame, but I don't want you padding the days, either." He spoke seriously, and honestly didn't seem to realize he was being insulting. "If it takes less time than we contract for, we can prorate the bill, right?"

Shelby opened her mouth and Ty hoped she'd tell this guy to get a fucking clue, but instead she said, "There's a possibility that it might take longer than thirty days, and it won't be because I'm padding the days."

"How much riding experience do you have?" Ty asked Blake.

Shelby shot him a sharp look, but he ignored it.

"I've been riding since I was twelve."

"Horses like... Evarado, here?" If Shelby had laser eyes, he would have been dead by now, but he wanted to know how "tame" this horse had to be.

In other words, what kind of miracle did these people expect and was Shelby seriously going to tackle this.

"He's been spoiled and allowed to become headstrong. He just needs to learn who is boss," Paul said, slipping an arm around Blake's shoulders.

So Paul understood the deal with the horse, but he didn't seem to understand that rehabilitating the horse wasn't like fixing a malfunctioning vehicle. He couldn't just replace a chip and drive away safely.

"Why don't we step into the house and take a look at the

contract," Shelby said smoothly.

Ty let out a breath and then leaned his forearms on the fence rails as Shelby guided the couple to the house. The horse snorted at him and started pawing the dirt.

He didn't like this, but there wasn't a hell of a lot he could do about it. He had faith in Shelby's abilities, but he'd dealt with enough rank horses to know that this one could be trouble. Not because he was mean, but because he was spoiled and he was insecure. Fear was a mighty motivating factor for horses and when horses got scared, they acted on pure instinct.

Kind of like some people he knew.

Ten minutes later, Shelby, Paul, and Blake came back out of the house and walked toward Paul's shiny new truck. Blake went to the fence, said goodbye to the black gelding, and urged him to be a good boy for Shelby. The horse snorted and Ty felt like doing the same.

"I'll be in touch," Paul said before guiding Blake to the truck and opening the door for her. She climbed inside and arranged herself in the middle seat next to where Paul would sit.

"I'll let you know what I think in a few days," Shelby replied as he got into his truck.

Blake waved and Paul started the engine.

"Do you get a lot of clients like that?" Ty asked as the blue truck and trailer rolled down the driveway. Because he'd much rather deal with a rank horse than a privileged yet clueless client. Shelby now had both.

She kept her eyes on the lights of the truck. "Believe it or not, they are not unique."

"You have more patience than I do."

"In some ways."

The horse let out a shrill whinny and was answered by almost every animal on the place.

Ty shook his head. "You probably know what I'm going to say next."

"You think I should be careful with this horse." She turned her head to meet his gaze.

"Something along those lines."

"I plan to work him in the late afternoon. After you guys are home."

"Do you want me to help you with him?"

She met his gaze and, for the first time since arriving on the ranch, her expression held no hint of defensiveness. "I want you within shouting distance."

Ty gave a slow nod, feeling as if being in shouting distance wasn't enough of a precaution.

"You don't have to agree," Shelby said in a low voice. "Gramps is still a decent hand with horses."

"I'll be around." He didn't want her taking on that horse alone. He didn't want her taking it on at all.

"I appreciate it—to the point that I'm not going to tell you not to question my clients about their abilities."

"Come on, Shelb... you needed to know her abilities."

"I have a form they fill out and I'm capable of asking my own pertinent questions." She glanced down at her watch then back up at him. "I've got to go. I'm going to be late as is. Those guys were supposed to deliver the horse an hour ago."

"Your business in town?"

"A date, actually."

His gut tightened. It wasn't his business what Shelby did with her time, or who she saw. He'd given up the right to have any say in those matters four years ago, but hearing that she was going out bothered him.

"Someone I know?"

"I don't think so. High school teacher. New this year."

"So you haven't been seeing each other long?"

Shelby didn't clam up as he expected. "He hasn't been in town for long, if that's what you're asking." She studied the horse for a moment, watching as he pawed at the edge of the corral, then turned to Ty.

"Like I said, I'm running a little late. Thanks for helping out."

She turned and walked toward the house and Ty stayed where he was, leaning on the fence and watching her perfect rear end as she strode away. It killed him to think of her going out tonight, even though she'd no doubt gone out many, many times while he'd been gone. But now that he was back, now that he had to stay on the sidelines and watch a situation he'd essentially created play out... it sucked.

Chapter Six

S HELBY LIKED DAN Hamilton. She really did, but he didn't send her hormones into overdrive, as Ty did. He didn't make her want to find a dark corner and have him all to herself. He made her want to go bowling, which was exactly what they were doing.

Cassie was up, adjusting her stance as she studied the pins with laser-like focus. She took two steps, brought her arm back and sent the ball into the gutter. Cassie was one hell of carpenter, but she was really bad at bowling. And the beauty was that she didn't care. Her bowling partner, Jess Evanston, with whom she worked, smacked his forehead in mock exasperation as the ball rolled harmlessly past the pins.

"Do you mind if I give you some pointers?" Dan asked.

"Point away," Cassie said, laughing as she hoisted her ball up out of the return. "Not that it'll do any good."

"I have to try."

Shelby leaned back and watched as her date adjusted her best friend's stance. Jess caught her eye and raised his eyebrows as if to ask if there was a little spark there. She gave a small shrug in return. If there was, she was good with it—which meant she probably shouldn't continue to go out with Dan until she made certain they were on the same page—the friends-having-fun page. She didn't play games with people's emotions.

After bowling, they headed for Grey's for a beer, but the place was packed, as was FlintWorks, so they called it an evening. Dan took Shelby's hand as he walked her to her truck. She gave his fingers a squeeze and pulled her hand free. Dan took her retreat with good grace. Jess and Cassie, ever the carpenters, had stopped to study a new building façade a few yards from where Shelby's truck was parked.

"I hear your ex is back in town." Dan shoved his hands deep into his front pockets as he spoke.

"He is." Not what Shelby wanted to talk about, but the situation needed to be addressed.

"And living on the ranch."

"He's helping my grandfather."

"How's that going?"

"Good. Good." Her answer sounded positively lame.

"I... uh... what's our status, Shelby?" He frowned quizzically. "Friends? More than friends?"

"Friends for sure." Uncomfortable topic.

He smiled, looking somewhat relieved, which in turn made her feel relieved. "I like you, Shelby... but you scare me a little." The wry twist of his mouth took the sting out of the words.

Her eyebrows shot up. "Scare you?"

"A little. But in a good way. You rope. You ride. You can probably brand a calf."

No probably about it. She could and did brand calves.

Shelby pressed her lips together, then cocked her head as she met Dan's gaze. "Does Cassie intimidate you?"

He shot a look over to where she was good-naturedly arguing with Jess about whether the new façade on the building looked as good as the old. "I don't know."

"But you want to find out."

"Awkward, I know."

"Not at all. I think you should ask her out. She doesn't brand calves." She could build a house, though.

Shelby didn't think Dan was really intimidated by her roping, riding and calf-branding abilities... she thought he felt the same way about her as she felt about him. They were comfortable together. And decent bowling partners.

Dan shifted his weight and gave her a rueful smile. "I don't usually end my dates this way... you know, by asking if I can date another woman."

"People date to see how they feel about each other and I think we're going to be very good friends."

"Jess...?"

"Has been Cassie's best friend since birth."

"And that's all?" He spoke as if he couldn't imagine anyone being around Cassie and only being a friend.

Well, Cassie was kind of gorgeous.

"He's also her tortured bowling partner."

Dan laughed and then leaned in to take Shelby's face in his hands and lightly kiss her. "Between friends."

Yes, it was, because she felt nothing but a sense of pleasant warmth. No sparks. No fire.

"Thanks, Dan." She pulled her keys out of her denim jacket pocket. "I need to get back to the ranch and check on my grandfather." She raised a hand to get her friends' attention. "I'm taking off," she called.

Jess and Cassie abandoned their discussion and joined Shelby and Dan to say goodbye and remind Shelby to drive carefully. She got into her truck feeling relieved she and Dan were on the same page. The only problem she could see was she'd lost her buffer. Not that she needed a buffer to handle things with Ty. Nope. Plain old honesty and resolve should do the trick.

But a buffer would have been handy if push came to shove.

TY AND GRAMPS left for work early the next day, so Ty could get back in time to be there while Shelby worked the black gelding for the first time. She waited until she heard the sound of the quad engines coming across the pasture before heading to Evarado's pen. Best case scenario, she wouldn't need Ty. Worst case...no telling.

Catching the horse in his small corral had been a challenge, since he kept swinging his butt around toward her, but once caught, he respected the rope, which was a positive. Too bad there appeared to be so many negatives. At this point in time, her job was to evaluate which behaviors she could correct and which ones were beyond her abilities… and then, if things played out the way she thought they would, to convince the newbie horse couple that this animal was probably too much for them.

She released the horse into the round pen and he nervously trotted the exterior, calling to the other horses. Only one answered him. The horse suddenly snorted and shied and Shelby turned to see Ty approaching. His pant legs were muddy to the knees and his shirt was unbuttoned, hanging loosely from his shoulders. Shelby forced herself to look away.

"Thanks for coming," she said.

"Not a problem." He looked like he meant it.

"You know I'm putting these hours on your time sheet."

He let out a breath that bordered on weary, but he didn't look at her. Instead he studied the horse, who studied him back. She waited and eventually he turned his gaze her way. "I may as well give the Les report, since I'm being paid."

Shelby bit her lip. "Is there anything *to* report?"

"Like you said, he seems a little under the weather, but he took it easier today and seemed better for it. How's his balance?"

Shelby frowned. "Good, as far as I know."

"I've caught him steadying himself a couple times. He says it's from standing up too fast."

"I'll keep an eye on him. Thank you."

"Any time. And you don't have to pay me to spend an hour watching you work."

"You could be doing other things."

"Suggestions?" Shelby shot him a quick look but his expression was bland and she wondered for a moment if she'd imagined the sexual undertones.

She was certain she hadn't. Her body hadn't fully processed the directive to put the past behind them and her senses still went into overdrive when he was near. So, in some ways, hiring him had been brilliant, since he could handle Gramps. In other ways, ways that involved her and her peace of mind, not so much. But conditioning took time and she needed to be patient with herself.

Shelby gathered up her rope and carrot stick whip. "I'd best get started."

She turned and opened the gate without waiting for a response. The gelding snorted and tossed his head. Shelby raised the coiled rope and the animal tore off around the pen. The sand was deeper in this pen, so he had to work harder to run, but it didn't slow him down. He shied as he spotted Ty again and Shelby had to scoot to keep from being hit. She raised the rope and got his attention again, sending him on around the pen.

After he'd completed at least ten laps, without once acknowledging her presence with a flick of his ear or the roll of an eye, she took a couple steps and waved her hands, reversing his course. This surprised him. He was running to escape and now his direction had been controlled. The gelding shot her a quick look then once again focused on escape.

It was going to be a long hour.

By the end of the session, the gelding was coming to grips with the idea that she was the boss, that she made him run when he wanted to stop, that she changed his direction of movement whenever she pleased.

He snorted threateningly whenever she brought him to a halt and approached, but finally, just as the sun was going down, he allowed her to touch his shoulder with the end of the whip and then her hand without bolting. When she reached for the halter to attach the lead rope, he snorted and took off, then stopped and faced her. Shelby approached quietly and clipped the lead rope onto his halter and the gelding instantly sat back on his haunches.

"Fine," Shelby muttered, moving forward and tossing the rope loosely over the horse's neck to get it off the ground. "Have it your way." She raised her hand and sent the gelding back around the pen.

TY SHOOK HIS head as the gelding raced by. He hoped Shelby would be able to end the session before dark, but knew she couldn't stop until she was the winner of this round. If she did, she'd set back her training and she wouldn't do that. He glanced up at the automatic sodium light mounted to the pole next to the round pen. It was already starting to glow pale blue.

Come on, buddy. He silently willed the horse. *Do what you're supposed to do.*

After a few rounds and a change of direction, Shelby once again approached the gelding, who was breathing hard. This time he allowed her to rub his face. She unsnapped the lead, snapped it back on again. The horse didn't move until she put pressure on the rope and then he stepped forward cautiously. Ty opened the gate and she led Evarado through, taking him straight to his pen. Once inside, the gelding waited until she'd unfastened the rope halter, then jerked his head up, yanking his nose out of the halter before he whirled on his haunches and shot across the small pen, nearly taking Shelby's arm off in the process.

She rubbed her shoulder, then started coiling the rope.

"I can see what our next lesson will be," she muttered.

"Are you okay?"

"A little irritated to end things like this when it's too dark to do anything about it."

His mouth flattened. "I meant your shoulder."

"It's fine." She rolled it as if to prove her point. "Still in the socket anyway."

"I can't say I feel great about that horse."

"Early days."

"He's scared, Shelby." As if she didn't know that, but he wanted her to think about it.

Scared horses were dangerous horses. At the level at which he rode, the horses were seasoned professionals, just as he was. They seemed to enjoy the challenge of trying to dislodge the man from their back. It was their job, and often, after the whistle blew, they stopped bucking and started looking for the gate. But coming up through the ranks, competing at smaller rodeos, he'd drawn fresh broncs, new to the rodeo. Horses that didn't know what was happening, or what was expected of them—those horses could hurt a guy.

"My job is to help him move past his fear."

"I hope your arm remains in its socket."

"We'll work on it." She glanced over at him. "I have roping practice tomorrow, so I need to start earlier."

"I'll see if the boss will let me off."

"I'm pretty certain she will. I'll tell Gramps to cut it short."

"So... you and Wyatt Marshall have an entry in the Copper Mountain rodeo?"

"Thanks to Wyatt, we do." She gave a small shrug. "It's time for me to face my demons. I tell myself that I'm cool with screwing up"—her mouth twisted sideways—"and sometimes I believe it."

"I know that feeling."

"I'm sure you do."

"Is that a jab?"

"Maybe," she said with a half-smile.

It felt good to be semi-bantering, but it also felt a touch dangerous.

She gave him a serious look then. "I never in a thousand years thought you'd be back here on this ranch. Never thought I'd be the person who invited you here, but I think this might work out okay."

"So far, so good."

She stopped walking and turned to face him. "I'm curious... not that it changes anything now... but if you had it to do over again... would you make the same decision?"

So much for starting fresh. "I could lie and tell you 'no'."

"So that's a 'yes'."

Yeah, it was and he was sorry it hurt her. "I had to get it out of my system."

"At my expense."

"I had my own demons to slay."

"At my expense." She repeated.

"I wouldn't have been any good to you had I stayed."

"I think you could have been... you just didn't want to badly enough."

"I'm not going to crawl to you on my belly, Shelby." Which was a lie, because he was close to doing that now.

Letting things go, starting fresh, had been his idea, but he could see now that it wasn't realistic. They had too many things to talk about, too many deep hurts to address. If they didn't, then Shelby wouldn't purposely be picking a fight with him right now.

"I don't want you to crawl." She sounded surprised at the idea, which was total bullshit.

"Are you sure?"

She held his eyes for the longest time, her frown deepening before she said, "No. Maybe not."

"Thank you for the honesty." The words sounded hollow.

Shelby dropped her gaze, studied the ground near her boots for a moment. Her voice had a husky edge when she finally said, "I haven't been honest."

"How so?"

She met his eyes in a serious way. "I can't let things go, because they hurt like hell and I haven't worked through them. I can't say that I'm not still attracted to you, because I am."

"That's a bad thing?" He wanted so badly to reach out to her, pull her close.

Kiss her the way he'd wanted to kiss her when he walked back onto this ranch over a week ago.

"I don't trust you. I don't know that I ever will."

"What do we do about that?"

She gave a scoffing laugh. "What can we do? We figure out a way to coexist."

"Do you think we can do that?"

"We have no choice if you're going to stay in the area."

LES WAS QUIET as he and Ty loaded the tools before going to work the next morning, which suited Ty, because he didn't feel like talking. He had no idea what was eating at Les, but Ty knew what was eating at him. Shelby pretty much said she still cared for him, but couldn't, or wouldn't allow herself, to trust him.

They couldn't have a relationship without trust.

He and Les worked in silence until it was time for lunch and then they sat on their respective four-wheelers, eating sandwiches, until Les finally let loose with an actual question.

"What do you think of that big gelding?" he asked as he wadded up his lunch bag and shoved it into the tool box.

"Probably exactly what you're thinking." Ty got off the four-wheeler and pulled a t-post off the trailer.

Les gave a snort of agreement and picked up his hammer. "Shelby's good. Has a way with horses."

"I agree."

Ty put the post in place and Les hammered. He and Ty had come to an agreement—Les would hammer posts until he started to feel it, then he would stop for the day. "She had a horse once that was all skittish like that. Worked him for a couple of days, then called the owner and sent it home."

Ty was glad to hear that. "So you're saying she doesn't have short-woman's syndrome."

Les sent him a surprised look, then laughed. "Yeah. I

guess that's exactly what I mean." He sat on the edge of the trailer and pulled a bandana out of his pocket to wipe his face. "So she'll be honest about her abilities."

"But you're still worried."

"I am."

Ty nodded and refrained from saying, "Me, too," knowing in Les's eyes he'd lost that right.

Les sighed and stared off across the meadow. "I don't normally worry about her. Not more than the usual amount anyway."

"You know how pissed she would be if she knew we were discussing her like this?"

"What she doesn't know won't hurt her." Les went back to the trailer and picked up another post. "When this fence is done, you're pulling out, right?" The words were more of an order than a casual comment.

"I am." Which was true. If all went well, he'd be back on the road after the Copper Mountain Rodeo.

"Shelby might ask you to stay on to help me out. Don't."

Ty choked back a laugh. "No worries there." He hit the t-post so hard he sank it too deep.

Shit. He reached out and wiggled the post. Pretty solid, too.

"You know… I didn't come back to hurt Shelby."

Les shot him a look, but said nothing.

"Do you think I would have made a good husband? Before I left?"

"You guys didn't have to get married."

"You're saying I could have just hung around."

"Until you two knew for sure," Les agreed.

"Maybe I did know for sure... then."

"What the hell does that mean?" Les spoke in a slow staccato rhythm, emphasizing each word.

"I couldn't miss that window of opportunity." Not with his father edging ever closer to depression as the farm fell to pieces around him.

But it wasn't only his father living through him that pushed him to leave... he'd needed to get the rodeo out of his system. He'd seen firsthand what happened to people who didn't. He didn't think a day went by that his dad didn't regret giving up his career.

Les's mouth quirked in a *yeah sure* kind of way and then he turned to drag another metal post off the trailer. Ty followed him and set the hammer down on the fender.

"I know Shelby thinks that means I put the rodeo ahead of her and, yeah, I did. But I wasn't ready for anything else. Had I stayed"—he gestured as his lips tightened—"it would have been a train wreck." He picked up the hammer again and then reached out to take the post from the old man. "And I think you know that."

Les didn't respond. The power of silence.

"Here's the deal, Les. I didn't have the maturity to commit back then. I do now. And you may have married your bride at the age of nineteen and been blissfully happy forever and a day, but I had to grow up a little, and I recognized that."

He turned back to the fence and started pacing off the distance to the next post. He was done talking. Les didn't say one blessed word in response. Instead he started the quad and followed Ty, and once they were at the new locale, he silently went to work. But he looked thoughtful, so maybe Ty had gotten his point across to at least one of the O'Connors. If not, then he would leave the ranch in a couple of weeks with both of them thinking he was a total asshole.

Chapter Seven

"I WISH I'D thought of redoing this depot," Cassie said as she and Shelby waited for their order at FlintWorks. She said something along those lines every time they met in the old train station, and Shelby saw her point. Not only was FlintWorks successful, it was beautiful.

"Somehow I don't think you have the resources of Jason Flint."

Cassie pointed a finger at her. "And *that* is the only thing that stopped me."

Shelby laughed and leaned back as the server set down the beers between them. She was doing a decent job of pretending everything in her life was normal. Even Wyatt had refrained from giving her grief at their last roping practice—which he would have done had he thought she had an issue. He asked about Ty. Seemed okay with her offhand reply, which she'd practiced on the drive over.

"Here's to a small amount of time off," Cassie said.

Between Shelby's roping and her full roster of horse contracts, she didn't have much free time, and Cassie's carpentry business was taking off.

"It'll be a busy week. Jess and I are making some last minute specialty pieces for a couple of the store front rodeo displays and"—she sucked a breath in from between her teeth—"Dan asked me out."

Shelby lifted her glass in a salute. "I'm glad."

"I was so-o-o hoping you'd say that." Cassie leaned back in her chair, her shoulders drooping in relief as she smiled at Shelby.

"I really like him, just not... that way." She decided to leave out the part where she scared him a little. "He's a great guy."

"But he's not Ty?"

Shelby set her beer down. "Why would you say that?"

Cassie leaned her forearms on the table. "Because I'm worried about you. Why on earth do you have him back on the ranch? Yes, I know he can handle your grandfather better than most... but was it the only solution?"

"No. I could have let Gramps hurt himself."

Cassie frowned at her, unimpressed.

Shelby thought about diving into an explanation of her "total immersion" strategy, but instead she reached for her beer again. "It's only for a matter of weeks. Once the fence is done, he's gone."

"You're sure?"

"That's what he said, and I can assure you he's never told me anything just because I wanted to hear it."

Cassie considered for a few seconds, and then gave a grudging nod. "I'll give him that."

"Truth hurts," Shelby murmured. Really stung, in fact.

"Then I hope you're equally truthful with him."

"I am." Now. And she felt a damned sight better now that she'd come clean.

"And with yourself…"

"You're brutal," Shelby muttered, "but yes. I'm truthful in all regards."

They'd barely finished their beer when Cassie got a text and then dropped her phone in her purse. "I hate to break things up early, but my mom is having a plumbing emergency." She rolled her eyes. "Sometimes it doesn't pay to be handy."

"But mostly it does."

"Right." Cassie started to open her purse again, but Shelby stopped her.

"Mine. Yours next time."

"Thanks."

They left the depot together, parting ways at the door. Shelby needed to get home anyway. She'd raced into town after her session with Evarado because she'd cancelled on Cassie the last time they were scheduled to meet for their weekly drink and didn't want to cancel again.

As she turned into the driveway she could see someone leading a horse from the direction of the barn toward the corrals. Strange, to say the least.

She quickly parked the truck and jumped out, crossing to where Ty was putting Evarado back into his pen.

"How did he get out?"

Ty turned toward her, his features shadowed by the brim of the ball cap he was wearing. "I don't know if he did the horse-Houdini thing, or if Les forgot to close the gate latch after he cleaned out the water trough."

"Why did he clean out the water trough?"

"Humongous dust devil came through, tossed debris everywhere. We scooped out all the troughs on this side of the barn."

Evarado started pacing the fence, then came to a stop in the far corner. "Glad you caught him before he hurt himself. You know how it goes—"

"The horse that gets hurt is the expensive one or the borrowed one."

"Exactly." Shelby turned toward the fence and studied the horse standing out of the light, his dark coat blending into the night.

He snorted, a sharp whistling sound meant to warn off predators, and stamped his foot.

"Isn't he beautiful?" Ty said in a fair imitation of Blake.

"Like you said, he's scared. I wonder what happened to him, poor guy."

"Does it matter?"

She shook her head. "I'll evaluate for another day or two and if I make progress and he doesn't seem dangerous, I'll proceed as far as I can with him."

They stood in silence, close, but not quite touching. Even so, she felt him. Felt his warmth, felt his strength. Wanted to lean closer, but didn't dare because she didn't know if she could stop herself from disaster if she got too close.

He touched her shoulder and her gaze snapped toward him as her heart leaped. "I'm not the enemy, Shelb."

Her body stiffened as she fought the need to touch him as he was touching her, a response so deeply ingrained in her that she was surprised she *could* fight it.

It was only when she forced herself to remember he'd left her and then come back expecting all to be well that she was able to say, "You're not the answer, either. You're... a distraction."

She felt his reaction, felt his hand contract before he let it fall away, breaking the contact she told herself she didn't want. More honestly, it wasn't so much a matter of didn't want as couldn't afford to want. Because she wanted. That was the problem.

"What the hell does that mean? A distraction?"

Shelby lifted her chin and explained. "You are a walking talking reminder of a time in my life when everything had seemed so perfect... before it all went to hell."

"Then why am I here, Shelby? On this ranch? Because even though I can handle your grandfather, you could have hired someone else."

He wasn't touching her, but he was close enough Shelby wanted to put more space between them. Maybe a few extra feet would calm the jangling of her nerves and thoughts. But stepping away smacked of retreat, and caring too much, and reacting too much, so she stayed planted exactly where she was. "I thought that if you were here... if we spent time together without being lovers, that it would change things."

"How?"

"I thought I would get used to you."

He frowned, showing he wasn't quite following and one corner of her mouth quirked impatiently.

"Like sacking out a colt. You expose him to the things that make him react and eventually, with increased exposure, he no longer reacts to them."

The frown turned into stunned lift of his eyebrows. "You were sacking out our relationship so you no longer reacted to me?"

"We don't have a relationship, but yes, that was the theory."

She assumed he was going to tell her what a stupid idea it was, because it sounded totally lame when spoken out loud, but that wasn't why she shifted her weight and swallowed dryly. No, that had to do with the way he was looking at her, with his eyes slightly narrowed as if considering options.

"Let's see how this is working."

"How so," she asked cautiously, not liking the look in his eye.

"Kiss me."

"What?" Shelby jerked back and for a moment she literally forgot to breathe.

His perfect lips curved just enough to tell her that he was totally comfortable taking command of this situation. "Let's test your hypothesis and see how it worked."

"Don't be a jerk."

He merely raised his eyebrows.

She straightened her back, found her voice again. "I'm not going to kiss you."

"Yeah?" His gaze still fixed on her mouth and after a few tense seconds, she automatically wet her lips. He sucked in a breath through his teeth. "Kiss me." This time it was a command.

A sane woman would have turned on her heel and stalked off to the house. A sane woman wouldn't have put herself in this position in the first place or expounded on lame-ass theories to the very guy she was working them on. But the truth was her hormones had been battling with her brain ever since Ty set foot back on this property and she was growing weary of the battle.

She wanted to kiss him. More than that, she wanted to show him he was not the one in command of this situation. This was her ranch. Her life... which he'd walked away from.

"You want me to kiss you?" Her voice was little more than a whisper as she moved closer and lightly placed her hands on the front of his shirt. His heart beat beneath her palms. He wasn't as in command as he let on.

"Wouldn't mind."

Bullshit. He wanted her as badly as she wanted him.

His pupils dilated, darkening his eyes as she reached up to take his face between her palms and pull his mouth down to within an inch of her own.

"Is this what you want?" she murmured.

His lips curved as his hands settled at her hips, his fingers pressing into her flesh as he eased her lower body closer to his. She felt his arousal, hard and insistent, pressing against her belly but the answering flood of heat was not as strong her anger.

"Well, then maybe you shouldn't have left." She dropped her hands to his chest and pushed.

He took a stumbling step back while Shelby folded her arms and silently hoped he fell on his ass. He didn't.

He cocked an eyebrow. "Can't do it?"

Not the response she'd expected. "When you sack out a colt, you don't move too fast."

His lips twitched at the corners. "Then how about I move real slow?"

Shelby's heart did a double beat. She loved it when he moved real slow... and she couldn't afford to keep thinking this way. She closed her eyes in an effort to center herself, drew in a calming breath. When she opened them again, he was there. Right... *there*.

"Ty—"

She barely got his name out before he took hold of her waist and gave a tug, pulling her body smack up against his own. Her breath caught at the sudden contact and then his lips were on hers, obliterating all hope of logic prevailing as his clever tongue welcomed her back into the wonderful world of things he could do with his mouth.

Heat, longing, and anger tangled together as Shelby fought for balance, fought for control. She was losing at both. She pushed hands into his hair as he nipped her lower lip, knocking off his hat, which bounced on the ground behind them. He responded by taking her lips once again in a searing kiss.

Lost...

Neither of them seemed to notice when he backed her into the fence, his body hard against hers, his thigh pressed between her legs. She welcomed the liquid fire that spread through her as his mouth began to blaze a sensual trail down the side of her neck and she gasped as he hit the sensitive spot in the hollow of her shoulder.

And that was when he pulled back.

And for a moment all Shelby could do was to stare at him, wide-eyed, as the reality of what she'd just done slammed into her.

"I don't think this theory of yours holds water," he said in a low voice, still holding her by the waist.

And damn it all, she almost asked, *"What theory?"*

Shelby pushed against him, not so gently extracting herself from his embrace. She thought it very kind she didn't once again try to push him back onto his ass.

Once she had some space between them so her brain could continue its journey back to normality, she pulled in a breath—very, very slowly, so it didn't shake in the same way her knees were shaking.

"Good point," she murmured, amazed she could get the words out in such a natural tone. And since nothing wildly brilliant occurred to her, she simply said, "I've got to go."

"You mean run away from reality?"

She flashed a hot look at him. "How are we to deal with this reality, Ty? By falling into bed?"

"We'd like to." He pointed out.

"No *duh*." And somehow the less than articulate acknowledgement helped her find the strength to draw herself up and attempt to set some boundaries. "But that won't be good for me. Therefore, we will not fall into bed." She took a step closer in an attempt to show both of them she had this, pointing her finger at his chest. "Things between us will be just as they were before we kissed. No— they'll be better, because the tension's been broken. That means we can be... normal."

"Whatever that is."

"We work together and that's it."

"Yes, ma'am."

Her lip curled. "Do not mock me."

"Shelby... the last thing I want to do to you is mock."

Again that breathing problem. She took another step back. Then another. Then she turned and stalked up to the house and let herself in the side door so she had time to recover before strolling into the living room and pretending nothing was amiss.

So now what?

Shelby paced through the kitchen—quietly so she didn't disturb her grandfather—angry at herself for allowing her body to call the shots instead of listening to her head.

Who was she kidding? Her head had been fully in favor of ripping Ty's clothes off and getting what she'd been missing for so long. If he hadn't pulled back when he did...

Shelby pressed the backs of her fingers to her mouth. Just a kiss. No clothing ripping. Just... a kiss.

But clothes-ripping had not been too far off.

She stopped at the window, pulled back the curtain far enough to see the lights of Ty's trailer were now on. Damn it, she still wanted to rip his clothes off.

Shelby dropped the curtain and opened the fridge to pull out a beer. Why couldn't anything go according to plan with this man?

Chapter Eight

GRAMPS WAS UP before Shelby the next morning and when she walked into the kitchen, he gave her a look that made her wonder if he'd seen her and Ty kissing. It wouldn't have been difficult—they'd been under the yard light near the corrals, in full view of the house. She'd simply assumed Gramps had been watching television as usual, and not looking out the window.

"Coffee?" he asked as she went to the fridge to get out the eggs.

"Thanks."

Gramps got up from the table, then made a grab for the back of his chair to steady himself. Shelby opened her mouth to ask if he was all right, but he gave her a warning look. "Don't."

As if she would let this slide. "Did you almost fall over just now?"

"I got up too fast."

"That's what you told Ty the other day."

"You guys are comparing notes... among other things?"

So he had seen. "The other things are my business."

"And my health is mine."

"Not when you're stubborn about it."

"It's only my knees."

Shelby set the egg carton on the counter and turned to face him. "Your knees."

"They aren't as stable as they used to be. They give. When they do, I grab things for balance."

"And that's it."

"Knees wear out." He walked to the stove and took the pot off, filling Shelby's cup with steaming brew. In about ten minutes, she'd be able to drink it.

"You could have them replaced."

"Not going to a hospital."

Shelby turned back to the stove and lit the burner under the cast iron pan. She couldn't blame him there. Her grandmother had gone into the hospital for minor surgery and died not long after due to an infection she'd picked up there. Her grandfather had never fully recovered from her loss.

"Then I guess we're at an impasse."

"Meaning?"

She glanced at him over her shoulder. "Maybe we both have issues we don't care to discuss at the moment."

"At the moment," he agreed.

He was only talking about her issues. His issues would be off limits forever if he could manage that. He sank down into his chair grimacing as he straightened out his knee.

Real pain? Or faked, to make her believe that his knees were the problem?

"Maybe you shouldn't go to work today. Ty can handle things."

"Maybe I want to go to work."

"That's a given." She cracked the eggs into the pan, then tossed the shells into the trash. "Tell you what... you stay home today—*just* today," she added when he opened his mouth to protest, "and I'll stop haranguing you about your health... for two, maybe three days."

Gramps frowned deeply. "Hard to beat an offer like that, but I'm going to work. Besides, this haranguing could work two ways. That was quite a show you two put on last night."

Shelby rolled her eyes, thankful her back was to her grandfather, so he couldn't see the color in her face. "Whatever happens between Ty and I... you don't need to worry."

Silence hung between them until Shelby flipped the eggs, nice and easy, the way Gramps had taught her to after she'd come to live with him. It had taken her forever to get the hang of turning eggs without breaking them, but she'd only been ten at the time and Gramps had eaten a lot of broken egg yolks.

She went for the plates, finally meeting her grandfather's gaze when she set the eggs in front of him. "I'm not twenty-three. I've learned some stuff since then."

Gramps didn't look convinced, but he finally gave a small nod and reached for the plate of toast he'd made before she'd gotten to the kitchen.

"And if any part of you feels bad, other than your knees, you'd better damned well tell me."

She had a feeling that mentally he was muttering, "Yeah, yeah, yeah," but he met her eyes and gave another nod.

Shelby held in her exasperated sigh as she set her plate on the opposite side of the table and took her seat. They ate in silence, and she assumed he was mulling over their mini-impasse. She wasn't going to let go of her concern over his health—and no way did she believe it was only his knees bothering him—and he worrying about Ty's departure breaking her heart again.

That wasn't going to happen, because she wasn't going to let her heart get involved to the point that it could break. Her instinct for survival was too strong for that. But heaven help her, she could see herself kissing Ty again... and more.

That was what happened when a woman had too long of a dry spell. The kiss last night had been both disturbing and amazing. If anything the chemistry between them was even hotter than before he left, which meant she couldn't screw around with this situation. As she'd told him—they'd act normal. Like two people who worked together. Now she had to make that happen.

"I won't be fencing tomorrow," Gramps said after mopping up the last of his egg with toast. Shelby looked up, so damned glad her grandfather had no idea where her thoughts were. "Meeting with my accountant in town. Thought I could visit the barber, too."

"I think a day off will be good for you."

Gramps gave a small snort of acknowledgement, then stood up slowly, as if keeping dizziness at bay.

Once he was on his feet, he picked up his plate and headed for the sink. "Something you need to know, Shelby—at my age, every day you can work is a blessing. And I'm going to harvest blessings for as long as I can."

TY CAUGHT A glimpse of Shelby heading to the corrals while he was loading equipment on the quad. He was about to intercept her when Les called his name. He turned to see the old man tromping toward him, looking as if he'd eaten an onion sandwich.

"Morning," he said.

"Morning." Les growled. "Is everything ready to go?"

"I have to get my gloves and water jug." Because Les was twenty minutes earlier than usual.

"Get 'em."

Yes, sir.

Ty went back to the trailer, grabbed his gloves and jug from where he'd left them on the fold-out table, then headed around the barn the opposite direction from which he came. He caught sight of Shelby at the tack shed, wrestling with the stubborn latch that apparently still jammed when closed wrong, and all he wanted to do at that moment was to help her beat the rusty fastener into submission, then turn her in his arms. Kiss her lips. Feel her soft skin beneath his fingers.

But no. Instead they would "act normal".

"What's up with Les?"

Shelby started, then swung her gaze toward him, blue eyes wide with concern. "Why?"

"He looks like he wants to deck me."

She let out a breath, looking relieved that her grandfather might want to hit him. "But he's not having balance issues?"

Ty frowned at her. "Not right now."

She brushed a couple of windblown tendrils off her face. "He saw us last night." She turned back to the latch, gave it a mighty twist and it opened. "Finally." She stepped inside, coming back out a few seconds later with a halter, rope and carrot stick whip.

"By 'saw us' you mean—"

She gave him an impatient look. "I think you know what I mean." She started coiling the rope, the picture of cool nonchalance. "He'll get over it."

Les might get over it, but would Ty? Shelby was all walled up, deep in the land of denial, and he thought about pointing out she was not acting normal, but it wasn't the time. He'd allow Shelby her walls. At least until he figured out a few things. No. Make that a lot of things. Maybe a bigger man could have pretended he was good with things the way they were. That he didn't still want Shelby back in his life.

He wasn't that big.

There was a loud clattering sound on the other side of the machine shed—the sound of posts being rearranged on a trailer by an impatient and protective grandfather. "Les is waiting."

Waiting and pacing. And he didn't look pleased when he saw Ty coming around the far end of the barn instead of returning the way he'd left.

"We have a lot to do. We're quitting early today so that I can be at the round pen this afternoon when Shelby works that knot-head gelding."

Les was going to be there when Shelby worked the gelding?

Ty didn't fight him. It would have only made matters worse. Les bristled at any suggestion he wasn't capable of doing what he'd done for his entire life. Ty figured he'd stay close, just in case there was trouble, and he was fairly certain there wouldn't be. Shelby knew what she was doing, and she wouldn't get on the horse unless she was certain it was safe. Or as certain as one could be. Horses could surprise the hell out of anyone. Blindside them.

As could other things in life.

When he'd come back to Marietta, he'd told himself it was to see whether he'd feel comfortable settling there after his career was over. Marietta was his hometown, after all. And if he ran into Shelby... well, he'd see how things went. That had been his rather vague master plan, but within twenty-four hours of arriving, he'd been at the Forty-Six. It'd been a long four years with no contact—well, none except for that first call when she told him not to call again. Told him to forget about her.

He'd tried. Thought he'd been successful. He'd focused on his career, moved on with his life…

But he hadn't. And the kiss last night had simply hammered the point on home.

THE WORKDAY TOOK forever. Les remained silent and distant as they set posts and strung wire and Ty had initially assumed it was because the old guy was angry at him and worried about Shelby. As the day wore on, though, he started to wonder if it was more than that. Every now and again Les would hold onto a post for longer than necessary, as if regaining his balance, or he would stare off into the distance, breathing slowly.

Ty pretended not to notice, but he planned to report to Shelby. Something wasn't right.

After he and Les got home that afternoon, Les made it very clear Ty was dismissed and not needed again until morning—as in, *don't bother coming to the round pen for the training session with the black gelding.*

Fine. Les was protecting his granddaughter in the best way he knew how, so Ty sat on the uncomfortable metal step of his borrowed camp trailer and greased his boots. Les might not want him around Shelby, but Ty imagined he'd be glad to have him around if there was a wreck in the round pen.

Ty waited until he'd heard Shelby successfully catch the gelding and lead him into the pen before he opened the boot grease can and dipped the rag in. The tack shed door opened and closed, bringing Ty's head up. She was riding?

No. Probably just tacking the horse up. It was standard procedure to work the horse with the tack.

He started massaging the grease into the dry boot leather. Arena dust was hell on boots, hell on hats, hell on the skin. It dried out whatever it touched and heaven knew he'd had enough of the stuff ground into him over the past years. But along with the dust had come silver buckles and some decent cash here and again. Bragging rights.

But more than that, it had given him an identity. He was Ty Harding. Two-time saddle bronc world champion. He had a purpose and a goal and he'd loved pursuing it more than almost anything else in life—to the point he didn't need the "World Champion" part after his name. Ty Harding, saddle bronc rider, was enough. But Ty Harding, three-time world champion had a nice ring to it.

Which was why he wasn't yet done.

He put the first boot aside and reached for the other. On the far side of the barn he heard the deep rumble of Les's voice and Shelby saying something in return, but no sounds of distress. Maybe the black horse had finally calmed down? He'd known horses that were sheer hell until they acclimated to their surroundings. Maybe old Evarado was one of those.

He hoped so anyway.

As soon as Shelby was finished with the gelding, he'd tackle the free weights. His shoulder was still weaker than before, despite Les was doing his best to toughen it up with the post hole diggers, and Ty's bad thigh wasn't even close to one-hundred percent strength-wise. But if his balance was there, and his reactions quick enough, if he could still read the horse, he could compensate when he rode next week.

No. He *would* compensate when he rode. And all his injured parts were getting stronger by the day.

He'd just dipped his rag in the grease can when the sound of a something hitting the rails of the round pen brought him to his feet. He dropped the boot, knocked the grease can into the dirt, and sprinted around the barn, ignoring the sharp pain in his bad thigh as he fought to keep from going down when he hit loose gravel.

When he rounded the corner, he saw Shelby mounted on the gelding, flying around the pen at breakneck speed. When the horse tried to slow, she booted him on. Ty came to a stop beside a pale-faced Les.

"Sonofabitch reared on her before her butt was in the saddle."

And now Shelby was schooling him. Horses liked to run, but they wanted to stop when they felt like it. This guy wasn't going to stop for a long, long time. As long as she kept his hind quarters engaged, kept him moving forward, he couldn't buck. If he *was* a bucker. Not all horses were. Some shied, some reared.

Regardless of tactics, a horse with an agenda was a dangerous animal, until he learned who was boss and until he trusted that boss to keep him safe.

Evarado was dripping sweat by the time Shelby allowed him to slow. Then she turned him and made him trot the opposite direction. When he started to bunch up, she kicked him back into the gallop.

"Stubborn," Ty said.

"Shelby or the horse?" Les muttered.

"She knows what she's doing." But Ty had to admit he wasn't a big fan of her doing it.

Finally, Shelby allowed the gelding to come to a stop and dismounted. Both he and Les knew she had to mount him again before she could call it a day.

Ty started for the gate and Les said nothing.

Shelby gathered the reins and waited. When the horse did nothing but roll his eye at her, she put weight into the stirrup, then stepped back down to the ground. The horse stood still. She repeated that several times before finally easing her leg over the horse and her butt into the saddle. She picked up the reins and the horse did a small jump forward, but he didn't rear. She allowed him to walk around the round pen, then stopped him in the middle and dismounted again.

Lesson over.

As she walked toward Ty and Les, her features were tight

and he could see she was exhausted. But she'd won that round. And the gelding didn't try his usual bolt for freedom when she let him go in his corral after untacking him.

"I'll be up as soon as I feed," she told her grandfather.

"Want help?" he asked.

"No. Put the kettle on and I'll be up in just a few minutes."

Les shot Ty a look, as if fully expecting him to jump Shelby the moment his back was turned. It would have been amusing if the situation had been different.

Ty waited until Les had crossed the driveway and was halfway to the house before Ty turned to Shelby and said, "Send this horse back. Now."

"Have some faith in me." Shelby moved past him on her way to the hay stack.

Ty caught up with her. "I know that *you* can ride that horse. My problem is that you're never going to be able to turn him into what those people expect, and by continuing on, you're risking yourself for a lost cause."

She rolled a bale off the stack and cut the strings. Ty pitched in and helped her load the hay into a large rubber wheeled wagon. She stood, wiping her forehead with the back of her glove. "I want to see how far I can get him, even if I don't get paid for all my days."

"Why?"

Shelby yanked the wagon handle, pulling it forward, leaving him where he stood. He caught up with her again, fully expecting her to ignore him, but instead she said, "I'd like to get him to a point where they can sell him to someone who knows what they're doing."

"Do you honestly think these guys are going to sell?"

"We're going to have a long talk."

Ty let out short humorless laugh. "Did you hear them when they delivered him? They're delusional. They want you to *tame* this horse—in less than thirty days, please." And anyone who didn't know the difference between taming and training should not be in possession of a horse like Evarado.

She shot him a fierce look. "I may not succeed, but I'm going to try. For the horse." She tossed two flakes into a manger. The horse shoved his nose in and tossed loose hay in the air.

"How about *not* doing it. For me?"

Her shoulders stiffened as she pulled the wagon forward, but she didn't look at him as she said, "You don't get to ask those things anymore, Ty." She stopped pulling and tossed a couple more flakes into the next feeder. "I train horses. It's what I do. And I'm not stupid about it. I know when an animal is too much for me. I can move this gelding to a better place."

"And probably get yourself sued."

"Meaning?" She tugged the wagon along to the next manger.

"Do you really think they're going to be satisfied with what you're able to do for him in thirty days?"

She fed the horses in the last two pens, then started back to the haystack. "He'll be a better horse when I'm done."

"I don't trust him and I don't want to see you hurt."

"You're a fine one to talk about getting hurt on horses," she said mildly.

"I ride bucking horses for a living. I expect them to explode. This gelding... you never know when he'll blow up."

Shelby's head came up. "Don't you mean 'rode'? As in past tense?"

He sucked in a breath and he saw the moment she understood that, no, he didn't mean rode in the past tense.

"You're going to start again?"

"I have an entry in the Copper Mountain. I'll see how things go."

For a moment she simply stared at him. "You'll see how things go." She echoed his statement flatly, but her eyes were blazing. "What. The. Hell?"

He frowned at her. "You never had a problem with my riding before."

Something flickered in her expression. "You've never been this beat up before."

"I disagree," he replied evenly.

"You walk like Gramps before a rain storm." She took a couple steps away from him, then turned back. "Son of a *bitch*."

She looked as if she was going to take him by the front of his shirt and shake him.

"What the hell?" she said again. Before he could answer, she asked, "How many times have you been hit in the head?"

"Twenty or thirty."

Her eyes went wide before she realized he was being facetious. "How many?" she asked from between her teeth. "For real?"

"Really clocked? Less than ten. Five times maybe."

She shook her head. "And the ground? What about that? How many bones have you broken?"

He scowled at her. That wasn't a fair question, given his occupation.

"So many that you can't tell me off the top of your head?"

"Some of them were small and barely count."

"Let's go with all parts of your body made of calcium, big and small, teeth included. How many?"

"Why do you care?"

She ignored his question. "I can't believe you're doing this."

"And I can't believe you're reacting like this."

Shelby pressed the heels of both hands to her face, shaking her head. "Neither can I." She dropped her hands and met his eyes again.

She was, in a word, angry. And he didn't get it.

"Why do you care if I ride?" he repeated. Because he was starting to feel a tiny spark of hope. After that kiss last night...

"Common sense," she blurted out. "What else could it be?"

"Maybe you freaking care about me a little?" he asked through his teeth.

"I care, all right? I care about you, but I also care about me. I care too much to take another chance."

His brow wrinkled. "Sometimes you got to cut loose and take a risk."

"I did. And the aftermath was not pretty." She lifted her chin to meet his gaze. "I ached for you, Ty. I'd wake up in the middle of the night wanting you so badly. It really, really hurt."

"Yet you never called me." Because he'd wanted so badly for her to pick up that phone and tell him it wasn't all over. They hadn't been ready to get married, but they could have worked at dealing with stuff together. But no. At the first obstacle, Shelby had cut him loose.

"Why? So that I could prolong things? Feel a little hope only to be smacked in the face by the truth. You were so focused on rodeo. On winning." She smiled ironically. "And it paid off. You became a champion."

"At a cost."

"Was it worth it, Ty?"

"Do you want me to admit I made a mistake? Even though we both had shit to work out and it probably wasn't a mistake? Is there something about hearing those words that makes everything better? Because, if so, I'll say them. I made a mistake. But so did you. I think we could have worked our way through things if you hadn't slung ultimatums at me. It didn't have to be all or nothing. Other people manage relationships while they're on the road."

"And how good are those relationships? How many people do we know that broke up because of them?"

"You didn't give us a chance."

"The only way I could stay sane was to have you gone once and for all. I couldn't handle having you pop in an out of my life." She glanced briefly down at their boots, which were only a few inches apart, then raised her gaze, her jaw tightening in the process. "Maybe you can operate like that. I can't."

"You didn't even try. I wanted to see you, Shelby, after I left. I didn't want to get shut out of your life."

"And you wanted everything your way. You wanted your life on the road. You wanted me."

"I wanted you *with* me."

Her mouth tightened ominously. "Same here. You could have stayed here. With me."

"Meaning that you wanted everything your way?"

"Low blow, Ty. I had responsibilities. School. Gramps."

"Les was well able to run things. Uriel was here."

"School. My future career."

"And what are you doing with your degree?" He was getting hot.

Angry. This wasn't all on him and maybe that was what

had been eating him for so many years. He was the bad guy, even though breaking up had been a mutual decision—in a way. She'd issued the ultimatum and he'd made the only choice he could have made.

"That's not fair, Ty."

"It's the reason you gave for not leaving with me."

"When I start something I finish it."

"Unless it's a relationship?" Another low blow, but he didn't care. "Given time, we could have built something."

Shelby shook her head and started up the path toward the house.

"You're a coward, Shelby."

She didn't slow down as she called back, "I'm a survivor, Ty. There's a difference."

Chapter Nine

S HELBY'S BREATH WAS coming fast and her heart was beating harder than usual as she approached the house, and since she had no delusions about her ability—or, rather, lack of ability—to hide her feelings when she was this upset, she veered away from the front door, which would take her through the living room and past her grandfather. Instead she entered the house through the side entrance leading to the mudroom and kitchen, quietly closing the squeaky door behind her. And there she stood, centering herself so she could act normal when she took the tea into her grandfather who would no doubt have a few words concerning the black gelding and Ty and who knew what else? She leaned back against the counter, letting her chin drop to her chest.

Next move, next move, next move...

She gripped the counter hard on either side of her, studying the worn linoleum as if it could give her the answer she needed. The linoleum remained stubbornly silent and finally she released her death grip when the kettle her grandfather had simmering on the stove started to slowly whistle.

Shelby poured the water in her grandfather's tea mug and dropped the teabag inside, letting it steep as she put a few store-bought cookies on a plate. Drawing in a deep breath, she carried the mug and plate into the living room where Gramps was sitting in his recliner.

He gave her a look as she set his mug on the table next to his chair.

"If you have something to say, I'm ready to hear it," she said as she took her usual seat on the well-worn sofa.

Gramps reached for his cup. "I don't have anything to say that Ty probably didn't already say."

She almost laughed. Gramps had no idea what things Ty had said, what subjects he'd broached. Or that he'd called her a coward. Her jaw muscles tightened at the memory, but she forced herself to relax.

"He has entry in the rodeo." Just saying the words made her stomach lurch.

Gramps gave her a startled look. "I thought he'd retired."

"He didn't." She picked up her cup to warm her hands, which were oddly cold. "He faked his retirement, and it really pisses me off. I mean, we both know he's hardheaded, but this is stupid."

"Maybe it's something he needs to do," Gramps said in a low voice.

Spoken like a man. "That doesn't mean I have to be around to watch. We've had our differences, but I don't want to see him get hurt." Shelby closed her eyes, did her best to shut out reality, but it refused to disappear. "Maybe you could fire him," she muttered.

Obviously her plan to get used to him by having him around was a huge fail. And now she had to contend with his riding.

"I would, but I need him—at least until the fence is done."

Shelby was surprised at his admission, but was careful not to show it. Gramps had just come very close to showing weakness. "I can hang on until then." Even though she was half afraid she was getting to the point that she needed Ty, too.

"We should be done a few days after the rodeo weekend if all goes well."

"Good thing," Shelby said matter-of-factly. "Because he plans on hitting the circuit again."

"And you don't like that." Gramps's gaze was just a little too shrewd.

"I can take it if he can." She meant the comment to come off as tough and uncaring, but the effect was ruined when her voice came close to cracking. What the hell?

Oh… she knew what the hell. She was scared. Scared of Ty riding. He'd ridden for years, but she'd removed herself from that realm, so she hadn't needed to acknowledge the fact he put himself in danger on a weekly basis.

She put her cup aside. "I'm going to town."

Gramps didn't argue with her. It was only seven o'clock.

Still early. There was no roping practice that night and she needed a couple of shots of decent whiskey. Drinking might not solve problems, but it dulled them in the short term.

"Are we going to behave?" Cassie asked when Shelby called to tell her that she was coming to Marietta for the evening.

"I hope not."

"Then plan on crashing here with me."

"That was exactly my plan."

SHELBY MET UP with Cassie at Grey's, where her friend had claimed their usual table near the billiard area. It was their tradition to have a tall beer and conversation at least once a month while they watched the cowboys play pool, either at Grey's or FlintWorks. But cowboys with pool cues didn't interest Shelby tonight, and it didn't take Cassie long to both notice and comment.

"I'm fine," Shelby replied.

"I don't think so." Shelby gave her friend a let's-not-go-there look, but Cassie, true to form, ignored it. "Spill your guts now or later. I don't care. But we *will* talk."

"You sound confident."

"Remember when I didn't want to talk after Tod cheated on me? You wore me down."

"That's different."

Cassie gave a soft snort, but didn't bother asking how it

was different. She focused on the game closest to their table while Shelby stewed.

Finally, without looking at Cassie, Shelby said, "It's Ty. He has entry into the rodeo."

Cassie set her glass down. Other than the first sip, Shelby hadn't touched hers. "I thought he was back in Marietta because he retired."

"Apparently he didn't get the memo."

"He *wrote* the memo."

"And we argued about it. The stupidity of him coming out of retirement." That was one of the things they'd fought about anyway. "It blindsided me and I totally overreacted."

"Of course it did." Cassie said, shifting her chair and leaning her arms on the table so they could speak more softly and still hear one another.

"I've been lying to myself."

"About being over Ty?"

"Among other things." She pushed her beer aside. "I can't go back into a relationship where I invest and get nothing in return."

"Don't invest."

"I don't think that's possible."

"Then own your investment." Shelby tilted her head to one side and Cassie said, "He did things on his terms. You do things on yours."

"I don't even know what that means." Shelby brought her forehead down to rest on her folded hands, then quickly brought it back up again.

Jason Grey didn't like it when people passed out in his establishment, or looked as if they were passed out—especially not this early in the evening.

"It means take what you want. Don't expect anything in return."

"I'm not wired that way."

Cassie leaned closer. "How are you wired?"

"I'm wired to give and get. And to not be left behind."

Cassie frowned at her. "Being left behind was your choice."

"It was my choice with Ty."

"I don't understand..." An expression of dawning understanding crossed Cassie's face. "Your mom."

Shelby gave a small shrug. "I have a thing about losing people."

"I can understand that, but... Ty rode broncs when you guys were together. Didn't that bother you?"

"Yes."

"Yet you said nothing—to me anyway."

"I refused to think about it." Cassie frowned at her and Shelby made a small gesture. "I never acknowledged that it bothered me." Not even to herself.

Weekend rodeos during the summer had been hell enough, but when he'd announced that he was going to be on the road full time...

"I was never okay with his riding. I... think I was afraid

of losing him. Kind of like I lost Mom. I've only deeply loved three people in my life. I lost one. I wasn't ready to lose another."

Cassie leaned even closer. "Did you let him go on purpose?"

"I don't know."

But even if she had, it didn't change the here and now. She certainly would never again ask him *not* to go. Now that she was older, and hopefully a touch wiser, she realized had he stayed four years ago, when he'd so desperately wanted to pursue his career, it would have spelled trouble for their relationship—exactly as he'd tried to tell her before. Ultimatums were not the answer.

And trust her to learn that the hard way.

She looked up at Cassie and sighed. "Cass... I think I still love him and I don't know how to handle it."

Ty FLOPPED OVER on the uncomfortable bunk, then sat up and leaned his head back against the jalousie window before scrubbing a hand over his face. He was still angry—almost as angry as he'd been when Shelby had told him to never call her again. When she'd shut off a two-year relationship just like that and he'd gone cold inside. Told himself if that was the way she wanted things, that was the way they would be. Fooled himself into thinking he'd moved past the anger into the realm of not caring about her if she didn't care about him.

He'd managed to fool himself until he drove into Marietta and had headed south toward the Forty-Six like a homing pigeon. But there was no happy ending waiting for him on the ranch. He'd hurt Shelby and she'd hurt him. He was willing to try again, but he'd been the only one in that frame of mind. Or rather, he'd been the only one until tonight. Now neither of them was in that frame of mind.

She wanted him gone and as soon as he got the fucking fence done, wish granted.

His phone rang, startling him, and he scooped it up off the window sill beside him, sitting up a little straighter when he saw his brother's name on the screen.

"Austin, what's up?"

Which was a better opening than which hospital are you in now? If his brother was in the hospital, he'd find out soon enough.

"Nothing good, that's for sure. If things don't turn around, I'll lose all hope of making decent money on this tour."

The tour being the International Bull Rider's Tour. Austin had truly hit the big time and he was all about going all the way.

"How badly beat up are you?"

"That's just it. I'm in better shape than usual."

"Has Dad been talking to you?"

"Only when I answer his calls." Austin hadn't been under the pressure to succeed that Ty had been at a young age. But once the old man had realized his younger son was quite possibly going to go as far or farther than his eldest, he'd started pushing Austin as hard as he'd pushed Ty.

"Are you calling for a pep talk?"

"Naw. Just to talk. Lonely on the road, you know."

"Where's your bevy of buckle bunnies?"

"Are you going to think there's something wrong with me if I say that I'm kind of finding them boring?"

Ty smiled a little and tucked a hand behind his head. "You're starting to sound like a jaded rock star."

"There are nights I feel like one. Have *you* been answering Dad's calls?"

"I have not." Because his dad was still all about him trying a comeback, and now that he was, he didn't want the old man to get wind of it. Not until he knew how things would work out.

"I have. Got me a nice little pep talk about the attributes of being a winner last night." He paused, then said, "He knows you're in Marietta. Someone there must have ratted you out. He pumped me for info."

"And you told him…?"

"You were looking to settle down post career. Not the right answer, by the way. He still doesn't believe you're truly retired."

"Continue to stonewall." Because Ty wasn't sharing this comeback ride with his dad.

If Ty failed, it was on him. If he rode well... it was for him. His father had driven him fucking crazy his last year, his first losing season after two championships, and had been crushed by the accident that had literally crushed his son.

"I have and I will. I know Dad means well, but I don't think he knows the stress he causes." Austin paused. "I kind of feel sorry for him."

Ty had felt that way for a long time. Irritated that his father wanted to control his professional life and sorry he hadn't had his own professional life to manage.

"Have you seen Shelby yet?"

Oh, yeah. Seen her. Had a fight with her. "Working on her place."

His brother laughed. "No shit? How'd that come about?"

"Les needed help."

"So are you guys...?"

Ty gave a scoffing laugh. "Hardly."

"You're just... working there."

"Yep." Ty debated.

He and Austin rarely bared their souls with one another. Instead they just kind of understood what was going on in each other's lives. But right now he felt like talking, even though he didn't.

The silence hung for a few seconds, and then Austin said, "All right, then..."

"All right."

"Well... good to hear your voice. I've got to catch up

with the rest of the crew."

"Austin." His brother's name popped out of his mouth. "Yeah?"

It took Ty a second to say, "Call any time... you know... if you need a sounding board or something."

"Will do. Thanks."

But he wouldn't. Ty was totally certain of that as he hung up the phone. He and his brother dealt with deep stuff alone and shared the superficial. Not the best way to handle things, but the way they were wired to handle them. He set his phone aside and stared up at the ceiling. Morning was a long way away.

He needed to move.

No. He needed to get out of this tin can and go to town.

SHELBY DID NOT spend the night with Cassie as she'd planned, nor did she get wildly drunk. Instead she drove home after finishing her one and only beer, with more on her mind than she cared to think about. Ty's truck was gone when she got there. He'd been in town, too.

Thank goodness she hadn't run into him. Her jagged nerves couldn't have taken it. Not after confessing her deepest fear to Cassie, who'd thought it was every bit as alarming as she did. How as it that Ty could do this to her? Show up after four years, turn her inside out? She'd been so convinced she was over him, but she was not.

She also could not deal with his lifestyle. The road... the danger...

The danger. She'd never fully acknowledged that before, telling herself Ty's career would soon be over and then they'd commence building their life together. And then he'd announced he was going pro. Even then she hadn't focused on the danger, but rather on the fact he'd chosen rodeo. Hadn't allowed herself to think about why she'd thrown down the rodeo-or-her gauntlet in the first place.

She didn't see Ty the next morning, because he headed out to start fencing before Gramps had finished breakfast and she didn't see him that afternoon after finishing up with Evarado because he got into his truck shortly thereafter and went to town.

In a way, admitting she still loved Ty made it easier to deal with him being around. At least she was facing reality instead pretending things were different than they were—or could ever be. The feelings the guy stirred up in her were crazy in their intensity. She'd told him she'd ached for him before... she still ached for him.

She'd been avoiding him before. Now he appeared to be avoiding her.

Better for both of them. Had he guessed how she felt?

She hoped not.

Two days passed. Ty left for work early and in the evening he drove away. Shelby went to roping practice. When Shelby heard his truck pull into the drive early in the morning, she fell asleep. Which meant she was getting as little sleep as he was. It was starting to wear on her and the sooner Ty left the ranch, went back out on the road, the better for her peace of mind.

Evarado was starting to settle, which meant he was starting to feel secure around her. He no longer pulled the rearing trick, but now he spooked and shied as an avoidance tactic. Despite that, the big gelding was kind of growing on her. She felt for him. He'd been handled poorly in his younger years and had been in survival mode for a long time. As had she. Maybe that was it. They were kindred spirits.

And maybe that was why Shelby knew the horse she heard nervously running the rails late that night was Evarado. She went to her window and sure enough, the gelding was pacing his pen, snorting and pawing. She slipped into her robe and quietly let herself out of the house and headed across the drive.

Ty was already at the corral when she got there. The sodium light popped and flickered overhead and the horse snorted again.

"Glad it wasn't a wolf or cougar," Shelby said as she approached the corral. As soon as he heard her voice, the gelding quieted.

"I'll go see about turning this thing off," Ty said.

"Thank you."

He went into the barn and she could hear him opening the breaker box. A second later the light went out. Evarado snorted again, then stood still, listening for the unfamiliar overhead predator.

"It's okay," Shelby murmured.

The big gelding crossed the corral and came to stand close to her.

Ty came back out of the barn. "I'll replace that before I go."

"I'd appreciate that."

The darkness made her feel safer. He couldn't see her face, couldn't read her. He propped his forearms on the railings a few feet away from her. The big horse was now quiet, so she had nothing to focus on except for Ty.

"I'm surprised you're home."

"Keeping tabs on me?"

"Not on purpose. I'm not sleeping well." And how was that for hanging something out there? Well, he could make of it what he wanted.

"Don't worry. I'll be gone soon."

"You could be gone now. I'm thankful that you're not— for Gramps's sake."

"I owe Les."

So she'd once said.

He kicked a little dirt with the toe of his boot. "I can't help wanting you."

The out-of-the-blue statement made her heart jump.

Tell him how you feel... communicate. See if you can work some of this out.

She couldn't. Too damned dangerous. He was riding again, heading back out on the road. Maybe at some future point... not now.

"I'm not faulting you there." Her voice was barely a whisper.

"Small mercies." His tone was dark. He pushed off the rail, keeping a healthy distance between them. "Like I said. I'll be gone soon."

Her throat thickened and she didn't try to push any words out. She nodded, not knowing if he could see her acknowledgement in the semi-darkness.

"Until then, I'll stay out of your way."

He started toward his trailer, the gravel crunching beneath his boots. "Ty." He turned at the sound of his name and Shelby took a few steps toward him, wondering why she'd been unable to leave well enough alone.

"Shelby... maybe it's best if you don't say anything."

"Why?" She stopped walking and folded her arms over her chest as if cold.

She heard his low exhalation before he said, "Maybe we should leave things as they are right now. I think that would be better for both of us."

She turned on her heel and headed toward the house, her arms still wrapped tightly around her middle. This was best. Definitely.

But if would be even better if she didn't feel this overwhelming sense loss.

SHELBY STARED AT the ceiling of her room for what seemed like hours before she finally dozed off, only to be jerked awake by the sound of her alarm. She swung her legs over the side of the bed and sat up before she gave into the temptation to flop back onto the pillows and close her eyes again.

Pushing her hair back out of her face, she got out of bed and went to the window, catching sight of Ty disappearing into the machine shed.

At least she didn't have to see him this morning. Didn't need to think about him telling her not to say anything. Not to make things worse. It was pretty obvious she wasn't the only one hurting. He'd come back to try to make things right. Why couldn't she let him?

Because she was so damned afraid of losing him. That had always been the issue. She dressed and went into the kitchen where her grandfather had the coffee waiting for her and it was surprisingly drinkable.

"The coffee had been sitting there for almost fifteen minutes," he grumbled when she sat down and pulled the cup toward her.

Excellent. Shelby cautiously sipped and then sipped again. Perfect drinking temperature. Maybe that meant the rest of her day would go okay despite a sleepless night. Gramps pushed the cereal box her way, then got up to take his bowl to the sink. "I need to get going pretty soon. Have to meet with the accountant again and do all the errands I've put off. Do you have anything to add to the grocery list?"

"Nope." Shelby set down the cup. "You won't forget to see Lucy, right?" Shelby had made her grandfather an appointment with the local nurse practitioner for a quick checkup. She didn't like this knee business and she wanted to know what the deal was.

"Right."

Shelby stared at him as he walked away. There was something in his tone that she didn't quite like—to the point that when he drove back into the ranch hours later than she expected, she put away the horse she was schooling and went to the house. She met Gramps coming back out the door.

"Ready to work the black gelding?" he asked as she turned to walk with him back to the corrals.

"Yes. What did Lucy say?"

Gramps didn't even try to hedge. "I didn't go."

"What?" She stopped walking, but he didn't and she had to jog a few steps to catch up.

"I'm fine," he muttered. "My accountant appointment ran long, so I called the office and told her I couldn't make it. She was backed up, anyway. Glad to have the time to catch up."

Shelby didn't for one minute believe that, but what could she do? Hog tie the man and drag him kicking and screaming into the clinic?

Tempting... but she'd need help for that. And her help would be gone soon.

"I'm rescheduling, you know."

"I wonder how far Ty got on the fence, today?" Her grandfather mused aloud as if she hadn't spoken. He leaned his forearms on the rails of the corral and stared out across the pasture to the break in the trees leading to the leased land.

"Nice avoidance tactic," Shelby muttered as she let herself into the pen and caught the gelding.

"At the rate we're going, he'll be done a few days after the rodeo."

And then Ty would be gone. Even if his ride at the Copper Mountain Rodeo was a total bust, Shelby knew he was leaving. Their last argument may well have been just that—their last. If it hadn't been, then he wouldn't be giving her such a wide berth.

It was what she wanted… right?

The session with Evarado went well, although it felt odd not having Ty there. It was the first time since she'd started with the gelding that he hadn't been within shouting range, as Gramps called it, and she decided it was because the gelding was starting to act like a horse instead of a rogue.

"He might turn out okay," Gramps said grudgingly after she'd finished her session.

Indeed, Evarado was showing signs of trust in the relatively safe environment of the round pen. She had no idea how the horse would react out in the big, scary world.

"I'll tell you what, though," Gramps continued. "He

ain't a horse for an uncertain rider."

"No. He needs someone he can't push around." Shelby waited until they were on their way back up to the house before she once again tackled the issue of the cancelled appointment. "I want to make another appointment with Lucy."

"There's no need."

"I know you have a thing about doctors, but Gramps, sometimes we have to face our fears because not facing them can have serious consequences."

Not what her grandfather wanted to hear. His expression clouded. "I know about facing fears. I've faced a lot more in my life than you have."

Probably true, because he had forty-some years on her.

There was also the small issue of her not acknowledging fears. Deep down she'd always felt skittish about Ty's career, but never allowed herself to examine the fact. Maybe she'd been afraid of jinxing things—afraid if she faced her fear, discarded it, then he would be taken away from her. And the roping—she'd acknowledged that fear, but until Wyatt twisted her arm, she hadn't faced it...

"I think maybe I have a fear of fears," she murmured as they mounted the porch steps.

"How's that?" Gramps opened the door for her.

She waved her hand dismissively. "Just thinking aloud."

He led the way into the kitchen and went to the fridge. "Well, we all have our fears, Shelby. Some we face, some we push down inside." He pulled out a plate of leftover pot roast and set it on the counter. "You're talking about this doctor business, right?"

"Right," Shelby said. Among other things.

"My issues with hospitals have a legitimate basis. All you gotta do is read on the internet and you'll see I'm right."

"But sometimes you just got to take a chance—choose the lesser of two evils."

"Exactly." He gave a curt nod as if the subject was finished once and for all, and Shelby decided it was time to back off. For now.

She dished up the pot roast, cut squares of cornbread, put honey, butter and horse radish on the table. Gramps carefully steered the conversation away from healthcare issues as they ate and described the rodeo displays he'd seen when he'd been in town.

"People are pretty excited to see Ty ride again."

Her stomach tightened. She wasn't one of them. She gave a small start when Gramps reached out to cover her hand with his.

"I know how bad Ty hurt you when he left." She nodded. "But you guys were really young."

"We were."

Gramps frowned down at their hands, her small one under his rough gnarled one. They'd been through a lot of life together. He'd taught her a lot of things. She had a feeling he was about to teach her something new.

"Just because someone has to... do something that's really important to them... and leave... it doesn't mean they didn't care for you."

"I know he cared, Gramps. Just not enough."

Her grandfather pressed his lips together. "And did you care enough?"

"What do you mean?"

"Did you care enough to let him go?"

She gave a small snort. "I let him go."

"And told him to never come back."

To her astonishment, Shelby felt tears starting to build. She blinked them back. "I thought... I thought he'd choose me." And when he didn't, when he chose to continue risking his life, she'd been afraid to have him in *her* life. Afraid of the potential for loss.

"Maybe he wasn't in a place where he could do that."

"I didn't want to lose him."

"But you did." Gramps gave her fingers a squeeze and removed his hand.

I didn't want him to die.

"Things could be different now... if you can find the strength to compromise."

Shelby's eyebrows lifted and she managed a laugh. "Are you giving me relationship advice?"

"Guess I am. Something to think about. Life is short, Shelby. Sometimes you have to take what you can get and be grateful for it."

Shelby blinked at her grandfather, not certain what to make of the conversation.

"Are you roping at Wyatt's place tonight?" Gramps asked, pushing his plate back.

"Uh… no. The rodeo grounds." Shelby got to her feet, took the plates to the sink and ran water over them while her grandfather put plastic wrap over the remainder of the pot roast. "I'd better get changed."

Practice was starting later tonight, so Shelby took her time re-braiding her hair and finding something clean to wear. *Uncomfortable conversation.*

And maybe more truth there than she wanted to deal with. She hadn't faced her fears. She'd tossed down an ultimatum in a passive aggressive attempt to make Ty choose a safer occupation. Would he have been happy if he hadn't ridden broncs? Maybe. But he wouldn't be the guy he was today.

Was that good? Bad?

All she knew was she'd handled things poorly. Out of fear. And now… maybe… she had a chance to make things right?

Or she could leave them as they were, let Ty ride off into the sunset. Pursue his new goal.

Enjoy the time you have with him.

There was a very real possibility that he wouldn't let her do that. That she'd shot him down one too many times.

When she came back down the hall, wearing her good

boots and clean jeans, she found her grandfather already nodding off in his chair in front of the television—like he never used to do before.

Maybe this was part of aging. Maybe her grandfather's internal clock had changed from night owl setting to early bird. And maybe his knees really were giving out. Maybe she was so worried about losing someone else in her life she was creating concern where there was none. Gramps wasn't yet seventy. Young, really, as far as old guys went. Milo Kenyon was approaching ninety and showed no signs of slowing down.

But then Hawksley Carrigan had passed when he was younger than Gramps.

And wasn't she getting morbid?

Shelby put on her hat, grabbed her gloves and rope and headed for her truck, then changed course and went to the machine shed instead. There was only one four-wheeler parked inside—the one Gramps rode. Her stomach automatically tightened. It was getting late and where in the hell was Ty?

Chapter Ten

WALKING TOWARD THE pasture, Shelby shielded her eyes from the setting sun, and squinted toward the gap in the trees. Nothing. No sound. No four-wheeler. No Ty.

He's a big boy.

And it was going to be dark soon.

If he'd broken down, he could walk back no problem, even if it was dark.

But if he'd rolled that damned quad, as could happen if a person wasn't paying attention... Shelby's stomach tightened even more.

Less than a year ago a person in a nearby community had died rolling a four-wheeler.

Heart in her throat, Shelby zipped her coat and headed for the remaining quad, firing it up and hoping the noise wouldn't rouse her grandfather. Odds were that Ty had broken down. In fact, the odds were so favorable for breaking down she wasn't going to allow herself to consider any other alternative.

Damn it to hell… what was happening to her? Ty comes back and suddenly she's a basket case? Her first thoughts were those of mayhem and death? That needed to stop.

The sun was well below the tree tops when she got off the machine at the wire gate leading to the leased acreage and undid the latch. She dragged the gate across the dry grass and, since there were no cows in the vicinity, she left it down before driving on.

She followed the four-wheeler trail that led past new braces, t-posts, and tautly struck wire. Gramps had said they'd finished the north side of the riparian and were working their way down the south, but she hadn't realized just how much of a job they'd already finished. Another day or two and they'd be done with both sides and then she and Gramps would be ready for spring and Ty would move on.

She followed the track away from the area where the land got marshy around the creek, rode over a small hill and half way down the other side she caught sight of Ty in her headlight, standing near the creek, hands on his hips.

His head came up as he heard the sound of the four-wheeler she rode.

Shelby gunned the four-wheeler across the remaining distance. Ty's quad was half sunk in a nasty bog hole. He'd been digging around the wheels, and his jeans and boots were muddy up to his knees.

Shelby shook her head. "I won't ask how."

His voice was deadly as he said, "Probably wise."

She got off her machine and they stood side by side for a silent moment, then she glanced over at him. "I can't help it," she said in a low voice. "How?"

"It was getting late and I wasn't paying attention. I was looking across the field and hit it hard."

"Why are you working so late?" It was almost two hours after his usual quitting time and he obviously hadn't been stuck that long, because he hadn't dug the wheels out yet.

"To get the fence done so that I can leave?"

All right, then…

She shoved her hands in her back pockets, ignoring his show of temper. "Want a ride back, or do you want to try to pull it out now?"

"Now."

"I need to call Wyatt." She glanced up at him after pulling her phone out of her pocket. "Why didn't you call when you got into trouble?"

"Manly pride," he muttered so low she could barely hear him.

Shelby made her call then put her phone away and propped her hands on her hips. "It's been a long time since we tackled a situation like this."

"Last time it was a tractor, if I recall." His voice had softened an iota.

"Gramps was so pissed."

Ty continued to study the four-wheeler as if it were the tractor all those years ago. "Someone should have been watching where they were going."

Shelby also kept her eyes firmly on the half-sunk four-wheeler. "I was distracted," she murmured.

Something about a hand working its way up her thigh. And it had felt so good right up until the tractor tipped drunkenly into the bog.

"I remember that, too."

The roughly spoken words made her insides tumble. Shelby let out a breath and turned and walked back to her four-wheeler. She did not want to dwell on how she'd been distracted the day they'd buried the tractor in a bog not that far from this very spot. Or the fact they'd made love afterwards.

She got the tow strap out of the milk crate, fastened to the back rack with bungee cords, and handed it to Ty. He hooked it to the front of the four-wheeler while Shelby turned hers in a circle, bringing the rear end as close to the buried machine as she dared. Ty fastened the other end of the strap and signaled Shelby with his hand. She moved her quad forward, the strap tightened and then the buried quad started moving. Ty signaled her to stop, climbed on the muddy machine, straightened out the wheels, then signaled Shelby to move again. She stopped as soon Ty was on dry ground.

Shelby got off her four-wheeler and waited while Ty unhooked the muddy strap and rolled it. He stowed it in the milk crate, then headed back to his machine and started it.

She waited for him to pull up beside her then started back the way she'd come, her headlight now cutting through the darkness.

When they got back to the machine shed, Ty parked next to her and shut off the engine. The building was dark, but light filtered in from the yard lamp just outside.

"Thanks for the rescue."

"I was getting concerned. I don't like it when people aren't where they're supposed to be."

His expression made Shelby wish she'd kept her mouth shut, but he didn't ask for clarification. "I'll try not to do it again."

Like he'd be there long enough to do it again. She started out of the building, then stopped after stepping out onto the gravel. "Are you going to town tonight?"

"Why?"

He spoke warily and Shelby didn't blame him. She moistened her lips. "I have leftover pot roast in the house."

He gave her a hard look. "After everything that's gone down between us, why would you invite me to dinner?"

"I don't know." She spoke the truth flatly. "Maybe there *are* things to be said."

"In front of Les?"

"Ten to one he's still asleep."

"This early?" Ty knew Les's habits almost as well as she did, having worked with him for over a year.

"Crazy, I know. I made an appointment for him to get a

quick checkup today, but he cancelled it."

"I think I'd be more worried if he kept it."

Shelby nodded. "Good point." Great point, maybe. She'd love to discover that she was concerned over nothing more than the natural aging process.

Ty shook his head. "I appreciate it, Shelby, but honestly? Maybe it's better if I don't."

"It's just dinner."

"No. It's not." He slid his hand behind her neck, his thumb caressing the edge of her jaw, making her want things she could not have. "This plan of yours... isn't working." He released her and took a step back, hooking his thumb in his belt loop as if to keep from touching her again.

"No. It is not." Her voice was husky. She looked down at the ground. "I was afraid something had happened to you tonight."

"It did."

"No. I mean something... serious." He didn't say anything and when she looked up, she found him regarding her with a thoughtful expression on his face. "I realized today that I need to face my fears."

He frowned at her. "What fears haven't you faced? You're roping again."

"Yes. There's that." She pressed her lips together.

Hard. Tried to come up with an easy way to say what she needed to say. There wasn't one. She had to face her fears, but she didn't need to confess them, because confessing them would only serve to screw with Ty's life.

"I've been stupid," she finally said.

"How so?"

"I've wasted time. With you."

His eyes went dark. "What do you mean?"

"I let anger and fear take control, even when I knew I was still attracted to you… and that there was still something between us."

Ty frowned at her, as if he didn't know what to make of what she'd just said, then he slowly reached out to take her into his arms, cradling her against his chest. "Damn it, Shelby," he murmured against her hair.

But his arms tightened as she slid her hands around to his back and hung on.

"I'm not twenty-three any more. Things aren't as black and white." She leaned back to look into his face. "I guess what I'm saying it that I don't need for you to stay. I need time with you while you're here."

And she did. She needed to feel him touch her, make love to her. Reassure herself that he was alive and well and with her. No one knew what the next day would bring, but they had today. She needed to get used to today being enough.

"You're sure about this?"

When she could feel him growing hard against her belly? Oh, yeah. She was sure. But she had a hard time finding words, even one or two, as she stared up into his very serious expression. This meant something to him, just as it meant something to her. Maybe their lives would never align, but they had this moment, and she was not going to waste it.

"It's a place to start."

"I guess we've got to start somewhere."

He studied her face for another long moment, as if giving her one last chance to bail, then lowered his head to meet her lips in a slow, heart-stopping kiss. Her hands moved up the sides of his face and this time she took off his hat without breaking the kiss, tossing it onto the four-wheeler rather than knocking it off. It hit the ground anyway.

He deepened the kiss, his tongue demanding her total focus, which was just wrong, because his hands were demanding the same thing. The light popped above them and then went out.

Ty pressed his mouth against the side of her neck, making her gasp as he hit the sensitive spot there he knew so well, then eased back and let his hands slide down her arms to her wrists.

"My place?" he asked lowly.

"Our only option," she murmured.

Ty led her though the darkness, around the barn and to the trailer, where he opened the door and ushered her inside. He crossed the room to snap on a small lamp, but Shelby gave her head a shake and he snapped it off again. The windows of the trailer were clearly visible from the living room where her grandfather might no longer be sleeping.

Besides that, she didn't need to see him. She knew him. Every inch of him and she was going to renew the acquaintanceship. She pulled her shirt over her head, dropped it on the floor behind her. She heard the pop of pearl snaps as Ty followed suit. Next time they'd undress each other. Next time they would play the games. Right now she needed him. In her. He hadn't even touched her and her breath seemed to be coming in ragged gasps.

And then his hands were on her. Big, warm, rough, and callused. She caught her lip between her teeth, closed her eyes as his palm skimmed over her naked flesh, cupping her breasts, reacquainting himself with her sensitive nipples. She was getting warmer, wetter, with each new caress, and when his hand slid down over her ass, dipping between her legs from behind, teasing her clit, she almost exploded.

She jerked back and even in the dim light, she could sense his questions. *Too much? Too soon?*

As if.

She narrowed her eyes, holding his gaze as she put her hands on his chest and started slowly backing him toward the bunk. When his legs hit the edge, she pushed. Ty went down, snagging her by the waist and pulling her with him at the last second. Shelby gasped and laughed as she landed on top of him. He kept hold of her and rolled and the next thing she knew she was beneath him. He laughed softly, then propped himself on his elbows and took her face between his hands, kissing her deeply. Shelby kissed him back, savoring the feeling of being trapped beneath his long, hard body. She broke the kiss, nipping his lip before and trailing her mouth along his neck and jawline, tasting the salt on his flesh, drawing in his scent before reaching between them to take his swollen cock in her hand. If anything it got bigger as she circled it with her fingers.

Ty rolled off from her, dropping an arm over her and pulling closer as he reached between her legs to once again explore her very hot, wet depths. He muttered something against her hair as he teased her clit, and his cock bobbing in her hand.

"Now," she murmured against his neck. Next time would be slow.

Ty did not need a second invitation. He put a hand on her hip and rolled her beneath him. Their hands met at his erection and together they guided him in. Shelby's breath stopped as he slowly pushed inside of her and then, when he hit the end, she suddenly gasped and bucked against him.

Her orgasm hit her hard, taking both by surprise. Ty stilled for all of a nanosecond before he started moving, his strokes long and slow as if he were savoring every second of being inside of her. Then he started moving fast, more desperately, and toward the end, he was hammering her. And she loved it. Shelby felt another climax building and just as he slammed into her one final time, she arched against him—hard—and the world around her shattered again...

Best damned shattering ever.

Shelby felt dizzy as she let her head roll on the mattress. Ty pulled in a ragged breath before he slowly lowered himself, collapsing on his side next to her. Shelby dropped a limp arm over his side.

"Next time will be more civilized," he finally muttered when he'd caught his breath.

She smiled a little. "I hope not."

Ty HADN'T INTENDED to fall asleep. He woke with a start, then stilled as he realized Shelby was still in his arms. Where she belonged. She raised sleepy eyes, a sensual smile curving her full lips.

"Again?" she murmured.

He laughed and she curled back into him. "Yeah. Again. In a bit." He pulled her a little closer. "Are you glad we did this?"

"Yes." She stretched against him, her smooth thighs pressing against his legs. "It wasn't like we could keep doing things the way we were. Pretending we didn't feel anything."

"It was kind of miserable." And he didn't want to go there again. He idly stroked a hand over her hair. "Do you want to tell me more about these fears that you're facing?"

"They're just… things I need to work through."

"Alone?" She nodded against his shoulder. "So what happens now?"

She ran her palm over his chest, idly playing with the

hair there. "We take things slowly. See what happens."

"No declarations? No commitments?" Because they'd been committed before and he didn't see where it wouldn't be possible to be committed again.

She looked up at him. "I honestly don't know."

"If you were to ask me not to ride—"

"I won't." The words popped out of her mouth instantly and he could see that she'd given the matter some thought. He could also see that she was dead serious.

She settled her palm on his chest and rested her chin on it. "I did that once before. I won't do it again."

"Are you sure?"

She smiled a little. "Yeah. I am."

There were still things between them. Things they weren't saying, things that needed worked out. And Ty honestly didn't know if they would ever be able to do that, but he was willing to live with the here and now.

He lifted her free hand to his mouth, kissed her knuckles. And damned if his dick didn't take notice that his mouth was at work. And Shelby noticed and arched her pelvis against him.

He pulled her up on top of him. They could—no, they *would*—continue this conversation later.

Chapter Eleven

O N THE MORNING of the rodeo, two days after Shelby
and Ty made love, Shelby set a cup of coffee beside
Gramps's breakfast plate, then headed off to the living room
to call Paul Barlow. She'd tried to call him twice before, but
he hadn't answered and he hadn't responded to her voice
mails. But this time the phone only rang twice before a
cheerful feminine voice said hello.

"Hi. Blake?"

"Yes?"

"This is Shelby O'Connor."

"Of course! How is Evarado? Is he coming along?"

Blake sounded so cluelessly happy that Shelby almost
hated to tell her the truth. "Not as fast as one would hope.
You see... he has issues."

"Yes. I know."

Okay... "He's nine-years-old, which means he's kind of
set in his ways. It's going to take a lot of time to get him to
where he's... trustworthy."

"Do you need to keep him longer? It's only been a couple of weeks, but if you think that more time would help…"

"It's not so much a question of time as temperament." Shelby waited a moment, to allow Blake to soak that in. "He's never going to be a sweet horse. The kind of horse I picture someone developing a close relationship with." Because Shelby had a feeling Blake wanted a horse that she could love like a dog.

"But with time—"

"Blake… he's never going to be a sweet, dependable mount."

There was a long, long silence, and then Blake said, "But he's improving."

"A lot," Shelby said truthfully. "And he could get to the point where perhaps you could sell him to an expert rider and recoup your money."

"Sell him?"

"It's something to consider."

Another long silence and then Blake said, "I want to do what's best for Evarado. Please keep working with him and we can talk again when the thirty days are up."

Shelby felt a surge of relief, right up until Blake added, "You never know… he might end up just perfect for a little time and patience."

"I'll give you a call when the thirty days are up," Shelby said.

At least she'd planted the seed—and gotten permission to carry on, with the owner knowing full well that selling might be their best option. That was huge and it put her in a better mood as she contemplated her day ahead.

Let's see—her comeback roping event, in which she'd either choke or she wouldn't, in front of a hometown crowd. Ty's comeback event, in which he'd either get creamed or not, before a hometown crowd.

The better mood began to stall out. Funny how the roping had seemed like such a huge deal when she agreed to it, and now it was more of a minor blip on her stress radar. And if, like Wyatt said, she roped best when she was worried about other matters, then they would catch that steer in record time.

Shelby came back into the kitchen and poured both her and her grandfather refill coffees. "I have to leave in half an hour so that I have time to warm up. Will you be ready by then?"

"I'll drive myself in later." He'd already told her that he wasn't going in early for the parade, which was a first, and he hadn't wanted to go into Marietta for the Friday night festivities either, which had her wondering.

"Are you sure your knees are up to driving?"

Gramps set down his coffee cup hard enough to slosh the contents. "I'm able to drive."

He'd gotten damned prickly and defensive since his near fall in the living room the day before.

"If your knees are bothering you," Shelby continued, "you shouldn't stress them with that stubborn clutch. You know you can catch a ride with a neighbor and then come home with me." That way she didn't have to go to the street dance if she didn't feel like it. Between her and Gramps, they were missing out on everything that made the Copper Mountain Rodeo weekend so much fun.

Gramps let out a disgusted breath. "I don't need a chauffeur."

"No. You need to go to a doctor. Maybe it's just a matter of getting a brace for your knees."

"Fine. I'll see a doctor."

Probably in six months, when he was due for a yearly physical with his behind-the-times doctor. Gramps had been raised in a family that only saw doctors when something was about to fall off their body, or they were prone and helpless, thus allowing someone to get them to the doctor. Obviously he wasn't going to see the nurse practitioner.

"Do you want me to hook you up with a ride?"

"I'll do it."

Shelby gave a nod. "Rodeo starts at eleven."

"I know."

"See you there?"

"If not, I'll see you when you get home."

"Sounds good." She picked up her coffee up and set it in the sink.

"I'll do the dishes," Gramps said gruffly. "Just leave them."

"Thanks." She went over to kiss the side of his head.

"And thanks for agreeing to driving in with someone."

"Yeah, yeah." He waved his hand, but when Shelby started for the living room where she'd left her gear he said her name. She looked back. "Good luck today, kid. And remember, no matter what… you're a winner to me."

Shelby kept that thought in her head as she drove to Marietta and crossed the bridge to the rodeo parking. So what if she embarrassed herself again? In the big scheme, what did it matter?

It didn't. But Ty's ride did.

Open mind. Open mind.

"Ready?" Wyatt asked as she approached the trailer. Ginger was already saddled and ready to go.

"As I ever will be." Shelby untied the horse, bridled him, and mounted. They headed to the warm up area and started trotting big circles, allowing the horses' muscles to warm slowly. By the time they were finished, the announcer was heralding the grand entry.

Two events and they were up.

Three events and Ty was up.

TY WASN'T NERVOUS for his ride. He rarely was. He was either ready or he wasn't, and he knew he was ready. He'd had no practice rides, but he'd worked out diligently and muscle memory was a wonderful thing. He set his gear down behind the chutes and started stretching. The team roping was about to begin, followed by the mutton busting. He had time to warm up nice and slow.

He purposely ignored the team roping event when it started. Told himself he wasn't going to watch—right up until the announcer called Wyatt and Shelby on deck. The he couldn't help himself. He found a place at the rail and realized his heart was beating faster. He was nervous for her—more nervous than he was for his own ride. He knew what it was like to be in a bad place in one's head. Knew how doubts could hamper natural ability.

The horse Shelby had borrowed from Wyatt walked calmly into position as she adjusted her loop, his ears pricked forward, ready to do the job he'd been bred to do with no unnecessary fuss. But of course Wyatt would have the best horses that money could buy. He was that good... and he'd retired a champion.

Doesn't matter.

And the funny thing was that since making love with Shelby, the "doesn't matter" feeling was growing stronger. The driving need to win it all one more time, to not be taken out of the game by a freak accident, wasn't as strong as it'd been even forty-eight hours ago.

The team before Wyatt and Shelby roped, racking up a respectable time and then Shelby and Wyatt rode into the box on either side of the chute. The guys manning the chute nudged the steer to straighten his head so he was pointed forward, then the chute opened and the big animal lunged out. Wyatt was on him so quickly that Ty thought for certain he'd broken the barrier. If he had, then this loss would be on him instead of Shelby.

The loop dropped easily over the steer's head and Wyatt dallied before the animal hit the end, swinging the steer's high quarters around and giving Shelby access to the heels. Before Ty could blink she'd thrown and pulled her horse to a stop, dallying and stretching the steer. Double heel catch. No penalty unless Wyatt had broken the damned barrier.

The crowd cheered and for the first time since she rode toward the box, Shelby smiled as she eased her horse forward, taking the wraps off her saddle horn. The steer regained his feet when the rope loosened and stepped out of the loop. After Wyatt had shaken his loop off the animal's neck, the steer loped to the gate at the opposite end of the arena. Shelby and Wyatt followed, coiling their ropes as they rode.

"I know what you're thinking, folks," the announcer said in a conspiratorial tone. "But the barrier was not breached. The time is good and we have new leaders—Wyatt Marshall and Shelby O'Connor. May I say, Shelby, that it's good to see you back in the arena again? And Wyatt… way to pick the prettiest partner here today."

Ty pushed off the fence as the next team loaded into the box. When was the last time he'd been that concerned over someone else's performance? Maybe that time Austin had drawn that widow-maker bull that had never been ridden. Odd comparison, but the truth was his heart was still beating a little faster.

The bucking chutes were being loaded with sheep for the mutton busting so Ty headed toward his truck. He'd catch up with Shelby later and congratulate her, but right now he needed to spend some time in his head. He idly rubbed his bad thigh as he walked. The muscles there were as good as they were going to get. Were they good enough?

He had to believe that they were. Had to believe this upcoming ride was his new start.

If he got creamed, what then?

Then he was going to be damned glad he'd chosen a small venue, a place where people knew and liked him, to test the waters. A place where his failure wouldn't be pasted across online rodeo blogs and news sites.

SHELBY SHOULD HAVE been walking on air. She'd conquered the mental block, proved that she was still the roper she'd been prior to blowing things at Nationals. *Proved* she could rope in front of a crowd under pressure. As things stood now, she and Wyatt were at number one in the standings. It wasn't a national title, but hey... she bit her lip to keep from smiling sappily to herself... she hadn't blown it!

The mutton busting started. The crowd hooted and cheered for the little guys clinging to the backs of sheep, but all Shelby could think about was the event following mutton busting. Saddle bronc.

Was Ty ready?

Was she?

Once upon a time, she'd loved watching him ride. But that was before riding had become her rival. So was that why she was so nervous? Because if he did well, then he'd once again leave Marietta?

After the issues with Gramps yesterday, there was no way Shelby could give up everything and follow Ty on the road—even if he asked her. So that left her exactly where she'd been when he'd asked her to travel with him four years ago. Without any real choice.

She hated it. Hated being wedged in between a rock and a hard place.

So what choice did she have, except to put on a brave face and watch the guy she loved try to conquer his sport all over again?

Maybe that was what love was… doing the thing that was hardest of all to do.

Shelby pressed her lips together and headed toward the crowded stands, spotting a few empty seats up high where the crowd was thinner. She owed it to Ty to watch, to see how this all played out, even though she wanted very much to retreat to her truck and hide out.

"Great run!"

She smiled and bumped fists with the kid at the edge of the aisle, smiling at his family as they chimed in their agreement. Heads turned and people waved. Shelby waved back, glad to have congratulations instead of sympathy, but at the same time wishing very much that she could be alone.

She moved a couple beer cans to the floor and sat on the uppermost row of the bleachers. Truly the nosebleeds. The tractor came into the arena and did a quick pass after the mutton busting and then the announcer encouraged every to get ready for saddle broncs!

The woman in front of Shelby was holding up her program and Shelby caught Ty's name toward the end before she lowered it again.

Four guys rode and two of them made the whistle. Good rides in the eighties. The stock was better than usual this year.

Just her luck.

And then Ty was on deck. Shelby recognized his hat at chute number five, as they brought in his horse. The horse reared and struck the solid metal divider with a front hoof before going back to all fours and Shelby's stomach tightened.

Great. His comeback ride, the one where Shelby had hoped against hope he'd get a horse that bucked well enough to give him a score, but not so hard he had fight on his hands.

Heaven help her, she was praying for a horse that would give Ty a mid-level score—high sixties, low seventies. High enough that he didn't qualify for a re-ride. Yes, she was a traitor, but she was worried about him.

Shelby swallowed and focused on the chute, where the horse had finally quieted. She saw Ty's hat as he mounted once again and then, before she was ready, the gate swung open and the bay mare exploded out into the arena.

It had to be a little one.

Small horses could be harder to ride than the bigger animals. They were more agile and, as was true of this particular mare, able to change things up rapidly. She bucked, spun, and twisted, making it difficult for Ty to get his rhythm, but somehow he did, answering everything that little mare threw at him and then toward the end of his ride, he pulled off his hat and fanned her.

Damn it, Ty.

Shelby's teeth were tightly clenched together as she waited for his smart ass move to give him some payback, but no. The buzzer rang, the pickup men closed in, one of them reaching for the flank strap and the other moving into position for Ty to grab hold and dismount. Once Ty's feet were on solid earth, Shelby let out a very long breath as she closed her eyes and allowed her head tip back, coming to rest on the post behind her.

"You okay, sweetheart?"

She opened her eyes to see the woman, whose program she'd sneaked a peek at, turned around and frowning at her.

"Fine. Just… relieved."

"Is that your young man?"

Shelby just nodded because right now, she felt pretty

close to throwing up. This was even worse than it had been before.

IT HAD BEEN one of those magical rides where everything—abso-fucking-lutely everything—came together. He knew as soon as his feet hit the dirt he'd be in the high eighties. Scooter Do, the little bay mare, had done her part and then some, and he'd answered her every challenge.

He felt like hugging the mare, but instead he saluted her as she loped by on her way out of the arena, then slapped his hat on his leg to shake out the arena dust and headed for the fence.

"Ladies and Gentlemen!" The announcer roared. "You saw it here, at the Seventy-Eighth Copper Mountain Rodeo! Mr. Ty Harding's comeback ride and what a ride it was. Ninety-one points! That's a nine followed by a one, ladies and gentlemen. The score puts Ty firmly in the lead. Let's show him how much we appreciate him sharing his comeback with all of us here in Marietta!"

The crowd continued to cheer and Ty waved his hat again and then slipped through the man gate.

He walked away from the arena, intent on getting to his truck when he could sit and process what had just happened, when someone called his name. He turned and saw his father walking toward him with Buck Creighton, a former bareback bronc rider and reporter for *Rough Stock World*, the online rodeo magazine.

Son of a bitch.

It was all he could do to not turn and head the other way.

"Helluva ride, Ty!" His dad slapped him on the back and Buck gave an approving nod.

Ty briefly met his father's gaze. "I'm... surprised to see you here."

"You didn't think I'd miss your comeback ride, did you?" He jerked his head toward Buck. "I figured people in the rodeo world would be interested, too."

Ty held out his hand to Buck. "Good to see you. It's been a while."

"Yeah, it has." Buck had interviewed him after his two championships and they'd bumped into each other on the circuit. "Your dad called and mentioned that you had an entry at the Copper Mountain Rodeo. I've never been, had a free weekend, so decided to drive over from Boise and watch."

"Hope you're enjoying yourself."

"Nice little rodeo. Now...do you mind if I ask you a few questions for the magazine?"

Ty shook his head and avoided looking at his dad, who no doubt thought he had made a brilliant maneuver. "Not at all."

"So this comeback ride... it went well."

"I'm pleased."

"You were a late entry. No press about the ride."

"I had close to a year off and that last wreck had kind of ruined me—to the point that, as you know, I announced my retirement. I wasn't certain that I'd healed enough to resume my career, so I thought I'd start with a hometown crowd—you know…people who are familiar with me and would have my back win, lose or draw."

"I think most crowds are like that Ty. You have a lot of fans."

"Thank you."

"You have a decent lead in the standings, but that can all change tomorrow. How are you feeling after today's ride?"

"Confident. My head's in a good place."

"Well, I wish you luck. I'll be here to watch that ride and I'd like to do another short interview tomorrow and perhaps we can work in time to discuss another matter."

Another matter? "Looking forward to it."

Buck lowered his phone and reached out to shake Ty's hand. "Good luck, man."

"Thanks." Ty shot his dad a look. "Catch up with you later, okay?"

"Sure thing, son."

Ty gritted his teeth and headed for his truck, certain his dad would catch up to him sooner rather than later, and sure enough, before he hit the entrance to the field where his truck was parked, he heard his dad call his name.

His shoulders tightened and he made a conscious effort

to relax his taut muscles before he turned back to face his father who was quickly closing the distance between them. His muscles he might have been able to control. His temper, not so much.

"What the hell, Dad?" The words came grinding out.

His father gave him a blank look, which only irritated him more.

"Did it ever occur to you that if I wanted publicity about attempting a comeback, that I would have arranged it myself? That I would have told you my plans?"

"What? You're pissed because Buck Creighton is here?"

"I'm pissed because you knew he'd be here, specifically to see me, and you didn't give me the option of telling him, no, don't come."

"Well, it's a damned good thing he was here for that ride. And I didn't tell you because I wanted you to focus on the ride."

"I don't know how you found out that I was entered…" Although he would hazard a guess that one of his cronies on the Copper Mountain Rodeo Board had clued him in. "But calling Buck Creighton, asking him to cover my ride, *without telling me…* uncool."

"Uncool or not, the guy was excited when I told him you were coming out of retirement."

"How did you know this was more than just one last ride at the local rodeo."

His dad gave a small snort. "I know you, Ty. You don't

do things like this for fun. You're as focused on winning as I was." His mouth tightened momentarily, as if he was deciding whether or not to press on. He pressed. "You've just proven that you're better than ever. You can work your way back into the money. Get your sponsors back."

A cowboy walked by, leading a horse with two giggling little girls wedged together into the saddle. Ty clamped his mouth shut until they were out of earshot. "This isn't the place to discuss this, Dad."

"I don't understand what we have to discuss!"

And therein lay the problem. His father was so heavily invested in his sons' careers that he didn't seem to understand they weren't *his* careers.

"Do you want to ride or not?" his dad demanded.

"On my terms." Which was the honest truth. "We'll talk later. I have to catch up with someone."

"Shelby?"

Ty stilled at the tone of his father's voice. "And if it is?"

His dad gave him an impatient look. "Don't be stupid about things, Ty. You don't have to settle, like I did."

And that was the end of this conversation.

"Later, Dad." Ty gave his father a curt nod and walked off, squeezing between two goosenecks parked side by side. His dad didn't follow and for that Ty was massively grateful. They would talk, once Ty had cooled off—in a week or so maybe.

Right now…

Well, Ty never had been one for public blowups and that was what was coming if his dad happened to catch up with him.

They hadn't made firm plans, but Ty had hoped to catch up with Shelby after his ride and to congratulate her on her stellar run. Now all he wanted to do was to get the hell out of Dodge. When he got to his truck he set his bronc saddle in the back and unbuckled his chaps. His dad hadn't followed him, but Ty wasn't taking any chances. He got into the truck, pulled his phone out of the glove compartment and dialed Shelby.

"Hey," he said when she answered. "Great run."

"Thanks. And I probably don't have to tell you that you were the best one here today." She sounded almost too enthusiastic—like she was forcing it.

Cool. Something to talk about later. "Can we catch up after the rodeo?"

"I have to help Cassie with some prep work for tomorrow's pancake breakfast. I don't know how involved it is."

"Then I guess I'll see you at the ranch later?"

"Yeah. Maybe we can go to the steak dinner and street dance... or something?"

Ty liked the idea of "or something", which would go a long way toward helping him forget about the shit his dad had just pulled in order to keep himself in the limelight.

Chapter Twelve

TY DROVE BACK to the Forty-Six shortly after talking to Shelby, feeling nothing but relief as he left the rodeo grounds behind him. He'd eventually seek out his father, make peace, but right now he needed breathing room. Les came home while Ty was feeding, parking his old truck close to the haystack and stiffly easing himself to the ground. His knees really were bothering him.

"Shelby said to tell you that she and Cassie are still working on something for tomorrow's breakfast," Les offered. "She'll see you at the street dance."

"Thanks."

Les stayed where he was, hands jammed awkwardly into his back pockets. "This isn't easy to ask but… are you two going to make each other miserable again?"

"I hope not." Ty spoke with utter sincerity.

"Me, too, because I kind of encouraged your suit with Shelby." Ty blinked, but before he could say anything, Les said, "I saw your dad there today."

"Yeah. He made the trip for me." And for him.

Les gave a slow nod. "You're going back on the circuit?"

"Yeah. I am." He hooked a thumb in his belt loop, as he always did when trying to ground himself. "But if Shelby asked me to, I'd stay this time."

"Why not just stay, even if she doesn't ask"

Ty debated for a second, then did something he rarely did. He let one of his deeper fears hit the light of day. "Because if things start to go south, she'll wonder if part of it is caused by my resentment at not getting one last crack at the championship."

Les didn't have an answer for that, and Ty didn't expect him to. Some things were simply too true to argue with.

THE TOWN WAS packed when Ty pulled in and he ended up parking a goodly distance from the blocked streets at the center of town. The band was just starting to play when he reached the main street with its banners, twinkly lights, and rodeo displays. He'd just started to work his way through the crowd toward the blocked off street corner where Shelby had texted him to meet her.

"Ty!"

He turned to see Tucker McTavish heading toward him in full-hug mode. She wrapped her arms around him, enveloping him in a lot of good smells. And she didn't move that far back after releasing him. "Congratulations!"

"Thank you." Before he could ask her how she'd been,

where she'd been, how long she was back for, she took his hand and pulled him toward the street.

"I love this song. Dance with me."

Ty allowed himself to be led forward. He liked Tucker and, unlike a lot of people, sensed her vulnerabilities. They'd had some good times before he'd hooked up with Shelby and they seemed to understand each other. All they'd expected of one another was companionship and good times. It had been comforting. Fun. Not enough.

Ty took Tucker's hands and they danced an easy two-step as he scanned the crowd. No Shelby.

"Are you in town long?" he asked Tucker.

"Time will tell." She moved closer to him. "I'm kind of letting things work themselves out." She flashed her beautiful smile and executed a spin, then came into his embrace. He loosely wrapped his arms around her, then gave her an apologetic smile as the music ended.

"I have to catch up with someone."

"Me, too." She touched his face. "Good seeing you, Ty."

A second later she was gone and Ty was working his way through the crowd.

"Ty Harding."

He stopped as he heard his full name drawled. Buck Creighton. Standing alone at the edge of the crowd, a drink in one hand. "You got a minute?"

"Actually, I'm on my way to meet with someone."

"Then I'd like to set up a time to talk tomorrow. After

your ride. I liked what I saw out there.

"It felt good." Ty jerked his head toward the side street, when the band started playing again. He'd lost sight of Shelby and would have to start the search again. "I've got a couple minutes now."

"We'd like to cover your comeback." Ty tilted his hat back. Not what he'd expected. Buck took a slow sip of his drink, watching Ty carefully. "Rodeo is a tough game."

Ty gave a small snort after Buck stated the obvious. "No shit."

"You've come back from one hell of an injury to ride for over ninety points and those were tough judges. They didn't give you any mercy points."

"I wouldn't want them."

"I know."

"We're making a documentary. *Rodeo Tough*. We'd like you to be part of it. Your expenses would be paid for as long as you're on the circuit. If you have a debilitating injury…" Buck shrugged, telling Ty he'd be on his own then. "We're showcasing a rider new to the circuit. One who's in the middle of his career and one making a comeback."

"That could be me."

Buck smiled faintly. "That will be you if you agree. Hell of an opportunity. Our dream is that you come back to win a national title."

"Mine, too." Ty shifted his weight. "How much does my dad come into this?"

"He called to tell us that you were attempting a comeback and suggested that we might want to write a human interest piece. Things snowballed from there."

"Good old dad." Buck frowned at his dark tone and Ty said, "He's kept an eye on my career. He was a rider once himself."

"I'm aware," Buck said. "Your dad had a lot of talent."

Ty nodded. He'd seen the videos.

"It's a shame he never pursued his career."

Ty saw no point in mentioning his father's bitterness had colored his life and the lives of those closest to him. Yes, everyone wished he'd pursued his career.

"You have some time to make a decision," Buck continued. "Day or two." He gave Ty a look that indicated he already knew what his decision would be. And why wouldn't it be a big fat "yes"? Getting his tour paid for and all he had to do was to let a viewing audience witness his victories and defeats—exactly as he did every time he climbed onto a bronc.

"I got to go and catch up with my assistant," Buck said. "I'll touch base with you after tomorrow's ride." He took a couple steps, then turned back. "One of my camera guys is coming in tomorrow to shoot some preliminary footage, but it's a just-in-case deal. I wish we hadn't missed today's ride, but the local crew got it on tape. Problem is, I have to pay them for it."

"What if I blow the ride tomorrow?"

Buck's eyebrows went up. "That's part of the game, son. You don't have to win it all for this film... but we'll provide you with the resources to give you a good shot at taking that title back."

Which was exactly what he wanted.

Right?

SHELBY STEPPED BEHIND a display of straw bales and adjusted the silk slip under the short dress she wore. The damned thing kept twisting and she was tempted to take it off, even though her borrowed dress was on the sheer side. The last minute prep for the Sunday pancake breakfast had taken so long that Shelby ended up raiding her friend's closet for a dress and bright red cowboy boots for the street dance. Because, damn it, she was going to the street dance and she was going to enjoy it. She was going to meet Ty soon and give people something to talk about and then she was probably going to kiss him goodbye in a few days. Her stomach was still in a knot over the ride. She didn't know if she could live like this—watching him ride with her heart in her throat... but maybe she could wait for him at home?

As if that would worry her less.

The one thing she wasn't going to do was to stop him from doing what he loved.

She stepped out from behind the display and stopped short as she almost ran smack into a guy. Her gaze popped up and she found herself face to face with Paul Barlow.

"Hi," she said in a bright voice, wincing as she realized it sounded a little too bright. Overcompensation was never a good thing.

"Blake told me about your call." Paul did not sound bright. He sounded angry.

"That gelding doesn't have the right temperament for someone like Blake." Shelby did her best to sound both matter of fact and apologetic, figuring a guy like Paul didn't want someone dictating the facts to him without acting sorry for reality.

He blinked at her. "You are supposed to fix that. You're a horse *trainer*. Right?"

Shelby pressed her lips together as she sought a way to explain so that he might actually understand. "Horses are like people. They have their own personalities and idiosyncrasies. Some are scarred by things that have happened to them in the past—"

"Horses are animals. Not emotional beings."

"Not true."

"You're making excuses for failing."

Shelby felt a flicker of anger, but did her best to suppress it. "I'm trying to tell you the truth about the situation—"

"Sounds like excuses to me."

"Because you don't know horses."

Paul sneered. "I know enough not to endow them with human characteristics."

Shelby pointed her finger directly at the center of Paul's chest. "I'm not making excuses. *You* bought a damaged horse because he was pretty and *you* didn't know any better. He cannot be *tamed* or fixed to the point that he's safe for Blake to ride, no matter how badly she wants to ride him. *He's not safe!*"

Paul gave her a withering look and was about to cut her down another notch when Shelby felt a movement behind her.

"You'd be well advised to listen," Ty said as he came to stand beside her. "She knows what she's talking about."

Paul let out a dismissive snort. "We'll find a real trainer, capable of handling Evarado. Blake will be riding him by the spring."

"You're a fucking idiot," Ty offered mildly. Color bloomed across Paul's handsome face, but before he could say anything in response, Ty added, "and in my experience, fucking idiots shouldn't own horses. That's a recipe for disaster."

Paul drew himself up. "You're out of line."

"And you're trying to put your girlfriend on a horse that could hurt her because you're too vain to listen to a view that's different than your own. The horse is dangerous and you're a fool if you don't listen to the truth."

He put his hand on Shelby's elbow and she agreed. This conversation was over. As it was, they were lucky to be on the peripheries of the blocked off street area where other than a few curious glances, they were for the most part being ignored.

"I'll be home Sunday afternoon. Come after six o'clock and I'll have a prorated bill ready."

"If you think that I'm going to pay—"

"Shelby has a lawyer in the family." Somehow Shelby kept from gaping at Ty. "Pay what you owe."

Paul exhaled loudly, then pushed past them. Ty watched him go, then turned back to Shelby.

"Nice lie."

"Easier in the long run. Besides, your great-uncle was a lawyer."

"He's dead."

"Details."

The music started again, a catchy country two-step. "You want to dance?"

"No." One corner of her mouth lifted wryly. "But if *you* do, I think Tucker's still around somewhere."

"Saw that, did you?"

"I did." Her mouth tilted into an expression that wasn't quite a smile.

He leaned in and took both her lips and her breath. "I don't want to dance with Tucker," he said in a low voice.

"What do you want to do, Ty?"

"I want to get out of here."

So did she. Shelby loved the yearly street dance and usually stayed until the end, but right now she was more than happy to slip away. This was not her normal rodeo weekend. Not only had she roped successfully for the first time in years, she was with a guy whom she loved, but didn't know if she could live with.

She definitely didn't feel like dancing.

They crossed the dark streets, the noise of the band fading as they made their way down a cross street, passing couples laughing and walking hand in hand. He waited until they reached a spot where there was no one around then pulled her down to sit next to him on a wood and iron bench. There was something in his expression that made her throat go a little dry. He looked... serious.

"I've got to tell you something."

"Yeah?"

He took her hand, lacing his fingers through hers before setting it on his hard thigh. "Buck Creighton wants me to be part of a rodeo documentary."

She stilled and his grip tightened on her fingers in response. "Wow."

"Yeah. I know. He wants to chronicle my comeback along with the starting career of a newbie rider and a guy in the middle of his career."

"Sounds like quite an opportunity."

"It is, Shelb. I won't lie."

"Are you going to do it?"

"Depends."

Shelby steeled herself, then did the only thing she could

do. "Take this opportunity, Ty. Finish your career."

Maybe she'd spoke too quickly, because he gave her a narrow-eyed look.

She frowned. "If you were ready to retire, you never would have gotten entry into this rodeo. You aren't done. You shouldn't be. You just rode for ninety-one."

He was still watching her carefully. Reading her. Shelby lifted her chin, met his gaze dead on. She didn't know why he rode, but he came back to it time and again. He'd been beat up, broken, crushed, and still he came back. It was ridiculous to stand in his way.

But this time she would not make him choose... she'd simply take away one of his options. She needed some time to work on the fear factor and he needed this opportunity.

"Trust me on this, Ty. It's best for both us. I have some things I want to accomplish, too. When you come back to Marietta... I'll be here."

For a long moment, he continued to stare at her, his eyebrows pulled together in a deep frown. He opened his mouth as if to speak, then closed it again. Finally, he said, "You're cutting me loose?"

"Not really," she said softly. "No anger. No recriminations. But I have some stuff I have to work through."

"Are you going to tell me about this stuff?"

"Once I get a handle on it." Or when he stopped riding—whichever came first. "Go ride your broncs, Ty. Get your championship. Then come back to see me."

"What the hell is this all about, Shelby?"

"Compromise, Ty. Pure and simple." She looked over her shoulder in the direction from which they'd just come. "I need to get back. I have to help Cassie."

Not the full truth, but she did need to get away. She needed time to think, but more than that, Ty needed time to see that she was right about the decision she'd just made.

"We'll talk later."

It was more of a command than a statement. "Yes. We'll talk later." After she had time to sort a few things out.

IN BUCK'S WORDS, it had been a helluva night. Between the offer for *Rough Stock World* to fund his comeback and Shelby essentially firing him from her life after they'd just gotten back together… yeah. Ty almost asked himself what else could happen, then remembered that Austin was riding the next day and decided not to jinx things.

He tipped up his beer and stared out over the river. As he'd approached the Forty-Six that night, he hadn't pulled in, but instead drove on to the turn-off to the illusive River Road that no one but locals could find. And there he sat, in his truck, pulling on a long neck.

He had a big ride ahead of him tomorrow. And regardless of what Buck said, he had a feeling it would matter if he blew it. There were other cowboys making comebacks. Maybe not all of them were former world champions, but there were some damned colorful characters out there. He needed to ride well. If he couldn't have Shelby, then all he had left was rodeo.

Ty emptied the bottle and set it aside, shooting a glance at the remainder of the six-pack on the seat beside him. Did he really want to get shit-faced the day before an important ride?

He did not.

He shifted his attention back to the river, resting his hand on the gearshift of his truck. He wasn't ready to go back to the Forty-Six, even though he knew Shelby had spent the night in town with Cassie.

He and Shelby connected in a way in which he'd never connected to anyone else—it had always been that way with them—but they didn't seem to be able to get past the obstacles life tossed at them. Didn't seem to have what it took to tackle things together... and he was just starting to get the drift as to why.

Maybe it wasn't the leaving that bothered her... maybe it was the job. She'd sounded so odd when they'd talked after his ride. And now that he was almost definitely going back out on the road, she'd cut him loose.

She'd never wanted to discuss his rides in the past. He'd tried a few times and got shut down. Maybe Shelby was afraid of losing him? As in forever? Like she'd lost her mom.

Had Shelby ever talked about losing her mom? Not many times. And she had never indicated in any way that it colored her life, but he knew it did. How could it not have?

People have a way of disappearing.

Okay... maybe she had talked. In her way.

Ty dropped his head back against the headrest, watching the dark water through half-closed eyes. He didn't know why he hadn't picked up on it before. It made perfect sense that a woman who lost her mother at the age of ten might have abandonment issues. Death was the ultimate abandonment. And Shelby hated showing weakness. She was a survivor, as she'd once said.

So what now? It wasn't like he could force her into a relationship. But maybe he could get her to talk. And... maybe he could talk, too.

He reached for another beer. His last.

Chapter Thirteen

S INCE SHELBY'S LIFE was wildly out of control, she roped with deadly accuracy. Once the arena dust had settled, the steer was neatly stretched between Shelby's horse and Wyatt's. The crowd cheered and Shelby's heart rate started approaching normal as she moved Ginger forward and shook her loop off the steer's legs.

"Told you that you wouldn't choke." Wyatt grinned at Shelby as they left the arena.

Their time had been even faster today than yesterday and the win was tied up. No one could touch them.

"Wish I'd done this at High School Nationals." But, unfortunately, her life had been pretty damned smooth back then.

Wyatt gave his head a definitive shake. "Things happened the way they were supposed to. Challenges make you grow."

Shelby snorted. "I'm tired of growing." Way tired.

"Tough. The process continues."

After helping Wyatt take care of the horses, Shelby headed back to her truck feeling... numb. The mutton busting was in full swing, and when the little guys were done riding their sheep, the saddle broncs would take over the chutes.

And Shelby had no idea where she would be when that happened.

Did she watch? Did she hide out?'

She'd leave. Her phone rang from inside the truck as she opened the door and she scooped it up off the seat.

"Shelby O'Connor, please."

Shelby's stomach tightened at the no-nonsense voice at the other end of the line. Whomever it was meant business. "Speaking."

"Trooper Russell, highway patrol."

"Russ...?" She'd gone to school with John Russell, who had the sad distinction of being the first trooper to respond to the Harry Monroe 911 call.

"Yeah. It's me, Shelby. Bad news. Your grandfather rolled his truck."

Shelby's heart hit her ribs. "Rolled... Is he okay?" she demanded. And when Russ didn't answer in the next split second, she repeated herself. "*Is he all right?*"

"He's being transported."

"He's alive."

"He's alive. I don't know the extent of the injuries. He was semiconscious when I got there. Where are you?"

"Rodeo grounds."

"I'm close. I'll swing by and get you. Three minutes.

Okay?"

Shelby nodded, only realizing she hadn't answered when Russ asked if she understood what he'd just said.

"I understand." Somehow she pushed the words up through her dry throat. "I'll meet you at the bridge."

"Got it."

"Promise me that he's okay."

"I'll be there in two and half minutes, Shelby."

TY CARRIED HIS saddle down the alley behind the chutes and tipped it up next to a small barrel, before pulling the chaps off his shoulder and shaking them out. The announcer had just declared Wyatt and Shelby the team roping champions and Ty told himself he was glad for her. She'd slain the beast. She was also killing him. Why couldn't they get it together?

"Hey, Mr. Hollywood. Heard you might have a film crew here."

Ty raised his head to smirk at Kevin Woods, who was currently second in the standings. "Rumors."

One guy hardly comprised a crew. He'd met with Buck earlier that day, told him he was ninety-nine percent sure that he would take the deal. And he felt good about it. Even if he choked this season, he'd have given it a shot, and Buck had indicated that there could be future openings at the magazine for someone like him. They hired people with name recognition and Ty had that. He and Shelby had their issues, but he still had his career. And that was what he was focused on today.

He straightened after buckling his chaps behind his thighs, catching sight of flashing red lights heading across the bridge toward town.

"Did one of the kids get hurt?" Ty asked.

The mutton busting was almost finished and while he hadn't heard any kind of commotion, he couldn't think of any other reason for a code red.

"Not that I heard, but there was a car accident," Deke Mahoney said from beside him as he adjusted the knee brace he wore over his jeans before putting on his chaps. "My wife picked it up on the scanner in the truck." He glanced over at Ty as if making a sudden realization. "It happened close to where you're staying. County road near the Forty-Six Ranch."

"No shit." There wasn't much traffic on that road—only locals. *What if…*

Ty was almost the end of the alley before he was aware that he was moving. He started toward Wyatt's truck and trailer, then altered his course as he saw the roper talking to a woman near the rail.

"Have you seen Shelby?"

Wyatt shook his head. "Her truck's here, so she must be in the stands."

"Thanks." But Ty still had a bad feeling about this. He

dashed to his truck, the overly-long fringe on his chaps beating on his legs as he ran. He unlocked the door and grabbed his phone, punching in Shelby's number. She answered on the second ring.

"What?" She snapped the word out instead of saying hello.

"Where are you?"

"Gramps was in a rollover."

Shit. Shit. Shit. "Local hospital?" He didn't want to travel to Marietta General only to discover that Les had been taken to Bozeman.

"I... uh... yes."

"Hang tight, Shelby. I'll be right there." He hung up before she answered and ran around to the driver's side of the truck.

"Ty!" He stopped at the sound of his father's voice. "What the hell? Where are you going?"

"Les O'Connor had an accident."

"You're leaving now?"

"Shelby needs me."

"You won't get back in time."

"Don't care."

"You *don't care?*" His father's face went red. "Buck Creighton is here. He has a cameraman. You have to ride." The pulse was beating in the vein in his forehead. "You being at that hospital won't change anything. Half an hour from now you *will* be there."

"I'll be there now." His father reached out and grabbed his shoulder as he turned toward the truck and Ty swung back. "I'm not *fucking* riding, Dad. This is *my* life, not yours!"

He shook off his dad's hand and jerked open the truck door. He started his truck and pulled out of the space, leaving his father standing exactly where he'd left him. He'd deal with it later.

Ty forced himself to drive slowly as he headed toward the bridge, then picked up speed after swinging out onto the street. The hospital was close and his dad was right—he could have been there in less than half an hour. Except that he needed to be there now. With Shelby.

TROOPER RUSSELL CAME into the emergency room with Shelby and guided her to the nurse's station, making certain she was in good hands before once again taking off. He'd barely left when the door swung open and Ty strode in, his chaps flapping around his legs.

"How is he?"

Shelby looked at the nurse, since she had no answers.

"You'll get an update as soon as we have information. Dr. Gallagher is with him now."

Ty's hands settled on her shoulders, big and warm and reassuring. Shelby swallowed and after giving the nurse the rest of the information she required for admittance, allowed

Ty to steer her to the waiting area.

He sat on a short vinyl sofa and pulled her down beside him, wrapping his arm around her. Shelby sat stiffly for all of two or three seconds, resisting… everything. The truth about where she was and why. The urge to allow herself lean on Ty. Finally, she gave up, closed her eyes to shut out her surroundings and settled her head on Ty's hard shoulder. His arm tightened around her and they sat. Silently. She was grateful he didn't offer useless platitudes. She didn't want to hear that Gramps would be all right except for from someone who knew for certain.

The waiting room was empty except for a mother waiting for her son's broken arm to be dealt with. Compound fracture according to what Shelby had overhead when the woman was talking on her cell phone. She was sorry a child was hurt, but bones would mend. Ty was living proof of that.

But her grandfather… what kind of injuries did he have? She was not ready to lose him. Someday she'd have to let him go, but not now. Not today. Ty's phone buzzed in his pocket for the third or fourth time, but he didn't bother to look at it.

Suddenly she sat up straighter and stared at Ty, who frowned back at her. "What?"

"You couldn't have ridden and gotten here when you did."

"I didn't ride."

It took her a moment to digest that small fact. He'd given up his comeback ride to be with her.

She gave him a cautious look as she considered the possible consequences of his sacrifice. "Even though you missed this ride, things will okay with the documentary, right?"

"I don't know."

"Surely they'd understand that you weren't thinking straight what with a friend having rolled his truck."

"It was more than my friend rolling his truck."

"But—"

He pressed her head back down against his shoulder. "This isn't the time."

But it was a distraction and heaven knew she needed one. She was about to mutter those exact words when the emergency room doors opened. Both she and Ty jumped to their feet as a doctor in scrubs approached.

"Sean Gallagher." He gave them both a quick nod. "Ms. O'Connor?"

"Yeah." She could barely breathe and once again Ty's hand was on her shoulder. He was there for her.

"Your grandfather doesn't have life-threatening injuries."

Relief slammed into her, making her knees feel rubbery and ridiculously weak. She pulled in a shaky breath, let it out again as Ty's arm tightened around her. Waited for the details.

There wasn't much to tell. Gramps was bruised and had some broken ribs and a gash on his head that had been stitched, but as far as they could tell, no internal injuries. He was also conscious and swearing a blue streak about going to the hospital—a place that killed people.

"My grandmother died from a hospital stay," Shelby said automatically.

"Your grandfather won't. But we need to talk about the cause of the dizzy spell that he had before wrecking the truck."

Shelby stared at him for a moment as his meaning sank in.

"Son of a *bitch*." The words came out before she'd realized she'd said them and she automatically muttered, "Sorry." Then explained. "He's been pretending his loss of balance was due to his knees. I should have pressed things. I didn't think it *was* his knees—"

"It's not easy to press Les," Ty said more to the doctor than to her.

"I know how stubborn some of these guys can get. Trust me."

"What now?"

"We admit him and observe overnight. I'll contact his primary physician, bring him up to date. He'll probably order tests, discuss medications."

"Good." Shelby leaned back into the hand that Ty had kept at the small of her back. "Will we be able to see him?"

"As soon as we get him into a room, sure. Just be aware that he's on pain meds and may not be all that lucid. He may not remember the visit. And he may be vivid in his language." The doctor smiled a little.

"I just want to see him." Assure herself that he was alive and well and then maybe yell at him for not telling her the full truth about his dizzy spells.

LES WAS A sight. Bandaged on his head and arms, hooked to an IV, and fighting the pain meds to stay conscious. The guy was truly afraid of hospitals and Ty had a feeling Les thought if he closed his eyes for even a moment, it might be for the last time.

"Gramps…" Shelby's voice was steady, but he had his palm pressed against her lower back and he could feel her shaking.

"I'm fine, baby girl."

Shelby pressed her lips together and shot a look at Ty before saying, "You only call me that when you don't want me to yell at you."

"Gotta do what I can to protect myself." His voice was low, his words dragged out.

The pain meds were winning. His eyes started to drift shut.

Shelby pulled in a breath and exhaled slowly as Les's head tilted to the side. The door pushed open and they turned to see Dr. Murphy, whom Ty assumed was Les's regular physician, come in.

"I see Les has been up to no good," the doctor said as he approached the bed.

"He's been having issues with his balance, but blamed it on bad knees."

"Sounds like Les. There are a number of things we can check, but the first will be his blood pressure meds." He settled a hand on Shelby's shoulder. "Whatever it is, we'll get it taken care of. Les is a tough old bird and now that I know he's having a problem we can deal with it." He looked up at Ty. "Nice to see you vertical."

Ty couldn't help but laugh. The last time he'd seen the good doctor had been after getting creamed at the 68th Copper Mountain Rodeo. "I'm doing better now."

"I heard that you're coming out of retirement."

Ty felt Shelby stiffen beside him. "Playing it by ear," he said.

Dr. Murphy shifted his attention to Shelby. "We'll let Les rest, run some tests in the morning and if all's well, we'll release him."

"But he's going to be okay?"

"Shelby… I promise you. Your grandfather will be back on his feet being difficult to manage within a matter of days. The important thing is to get him out of this hospital."

As they walked out of the room, Ty's phone buzzed yet again in his pocket and this time he answered.

"Yeah. Les is all right." He listened for a couple more seconds as they walked, then came to dead stop just outside the ER entrance. "Look, Dad, I don't care what you and Buck arranged, I can't—"

Shelby touched his arm and he shifted his frowning gaze to her. "Do it."

Ty lowered the phone. "You don't know what 'it' is."

"Do it."

She could see him fighting with himself, weighing pros and cons. He met her gaze then, his expression beyond serious. "Will you come with me?"

Her heart thumped. "F-for how long?"

"Just for today."

"I... can do today." Maybe she could do more than that.

Ty uncovered the phone. "I'll be there... yes, I'll damned well hurry, if you stop talking." He dropped the phone back into his pocket, took Shelby's hand and together they jogged for his truck.

THE RIDE WOULDN'T count. He wouldn't win the buckle or take home the check, but he was going to ride. An exhibition they called it, because of his record-breaking score the day before. He smiled grimly. After Buck and his father had interceded on his behalf, he'd probably humiliate himself and eat a dirt sandwich. He didn't care. He had one more chance to do what he loved and the woman that he loved was there with him.

For today. She could do today.

The horse he'd drawn was rank—a notorious bucker, which was another reason Buck had wanted Ty to ride. They hadn't had much time to talk before he was up, but Buck told him they could work an angle with Les's accident and self-sacrifice that would add depth to the documentary. Whatever. Ty was going to ride.

Shelby had stayed behind the chutes with his father and Buck while he tended to his horse. Once saddled, Pippin— which was a stupid-ass name for a bronc notorious for stomping the shit out of cowboys—snorted, rolled his eyes back as if to take Ty's measure, and then flattened his ears against his skull. The horse was a pro. So was Ty.

"Right back at you," Ty muttered as he climbed on board.

He arranged his seat, adjusted his grip, his left hand on the top rail of the gate to steady himself. Then the nod and the gate swung open.

Pippin blasted out of the chute, his front feet barely hitting the ground before he was in the air again, twisting and kicking. Whoa, shit. There would be no smart ass fanning of the hat on this ride.

Ty hung onto the thick rope rein and leaned back, matching his rhythm to that of the animal, only to have the horse change it up and throw in a spin followed by another twisting kick. Ty countered the movements with his free hand, never broke rhythm, although he tasted blood from biting the inside of his cheek after another jarring turn that knocked him off balance. He fought with everything he had to keep from touching the horse with his free hand as the whistle blew and he surrendered himself to gravity.

Yep. Dirt sandwich, but it was after the whistle and that was all that counted. As he got to his feet he heard the cheers, heard the announcer yelling about yet another great comeback ride, and all he could think was that he needed to get back to Shelby. He picked up his hat from the dirt, waved it at the crowd, saluted Pippin as he loped by with the pickup men in hot pursuit, then set the hat on his head and headed for the gate.

Buck and his dad were waiting for him at the end of the alley. His dad slapped him on his sore shoulder and Buck gave an approving nod. "I think this is all going to work out," he said.

"Yeah. Hope so."

"What do you mean hope?" his dad asked in an overly jovial voice.

"Depends on Shelby." He turned to Buck. "You said I have a day or two. I'll give you a final answer soon."

Buck nodded again. "Sooner is better than later."

"I won't tie up your time unnecessarily."

"I appreciate that."

His dad looked as if he had a lot to say, but Ty cocked a warning eyebrow at him and the words died on his lips. "I'll see you later, Dad. Buck."

He reached back to unfasten his chaps, freeing his legs as

he walked. His ride had been the last of the night and people were leaving the stands even though the awards would be given in the next few minutes. Always a rush out of the parking lot. Most of the riders were already gone, on to other rodeos or starting long drives home.

He pretty much was home... if Shelby agreed.

She was standing close to the main gate, looking a touch pale. She smiled as he approached, a taut, at-the-edge-of-breaking smile. He reached out for her, drew her close, breathed in the sweet scents of her hair and skin. Scents that somehow mixed so damned well with the arena smells he loved.

"Nice ride," she murmured against his shoulder.

"Thanks." She'd sacrificed to be here and now he needed to get her back where she belonged. He eased out of her embrace and took her hand. "Give me a second to collect my gear and I'll drive you back to the hospital."

LES WAS ASLEEP when they got to the hospital. After a quick look at her stubborn, sleeping grandfather, Shelby spoke at length with Doctors Murphy and Gallagher while Ty cooled his heels on the vinyl loveseat, idly rubbed his sore shoulder, and debated his future. Their future. When she finally joined him, she seemed to be in a better place, which made his heart lighten a little.

"Gramps was totally healthy when he had his checkup

with Dr. Murphy three months ago. But he got a blood pressure med for the first time and that's most likely the cause."

"Then why hide the dizziness?" he asked as he held the door open for her.

"Dr. Murphy is guessing it's because he didn't want to end up in a hospital."

"He was muscling through?" Ty asked incredulously.

Shelby sent him a look and he had to admit that he could totally see Les doing that.

"He was probably afraid that is he went off the meds, then he'd be a candidate for a stroke or heart attack, just as Dr. Murphy had told him he'd be if he didn't take the meds. What he apparently didn't understand is that there are other meds he can take."

"Remind me not to be that stubborn when I'm old."

Shelby shot him a frowning look, but he ignored it and opened the truck door for her. She climbed in without a word and Ty walked around the truck to the driver's side.

He put the truck in gear and pulled out of the parking lot, turning north instead of south.

"My truck is still at the rodeo grounds."

"I know. We'll get it in a while."

He continued to the stop sign, then turned onto the side street that would take him to Highway 89 by a circuitous route. Shelby settled back in her seat, her hands in her lap.

"You feeling okay?" he asked after turning onto the

highway.

"Better now that I know what's going on with Gramps."

He continued driving, past Harry Monroe's cross, which had even more flowers and mementoes than the last time he'd passed it. Shelby turned her head to study the sad memorial as they passed, then focused again on the highway in front of her.

"I'm taking you home the long way."

"I figured. I just don't know why."

But he did. And that was the important thing right now.

TY TURNED ONTO a county road that joined Highway 89 a few miles north of Marietta and continued down the gravel road. As soon as he'd made the turn, Shelby had known where they were going. Fifteen minutes later, they pulled to a stop on a small hill overlooking his family farm. Or rather the acreage that had once been his family farm and now belonged to a wealthy young couple who leased out the farming.

"Do you know what this represents to my father?"

Shelby held Ty's blue gaze and slowly shook her head.

"The wrong choice." He leaned his head back, staring out at the property with half-hooded eyes as Shelby studied his profile. "My great-great grandfather homesteaded the place. He grew grain to feed miners. Much smarter than trying to do the mining, but just as backbreaking. He was successful. He passed the land on and my great-grandfather and grandfather did well. My dad... not so much."

They'd never discussed the sale of the Harding family farm, or its history for that matter. It had been on the block when she and Ty had broken up, but Ty hadn't been living at home and it wasn't until after it sold that she'd come to understand that Kenny Harding had sold the place because he'd had to. He'd been going under fast. And then she'd thought she understood why Ty had been so reticent to talk about the farm or his father.

"Farming is a tough life," she finally said after a long stretch of silence. "Lots of people lose generational farms."

Ty rubbed a hand over his chin. "My dad gave up bronc riding to take over the farm. A big part of him died when he did that. The farm started slipping not long after he took it over. He had a couple good years and then the droughts came..."

Shelby set her hand on Ty's hard thigh. A moment later he covered her hand with his, squeezed lightly. But he didn't look at her. He was focused on the house and outbuildings at the bottom of the small hill. The place where he and his brother had grown up.

"He encouraged Austin and me to be rough stock riders from the time we could toddle. Sheep, calves, broncs, bulls. As we started seriously winning events in our teens, Dad started coming alive. It felt so damned good to see him be something other than morose and defeated. And Mom... she was so much happier when Dad was happy."

"So he lives through you and your brother?"

"Pretty much. I don't think a day goes by that he doesn't regret his decision to take over the farm."

"So you did opposite."

"I didn't want to end up a bitter person like him." Ty spoke slowly, choosing his words. "I thought I had to follow my career to avoid that."

"Why didn't I know this?"

"Maybe because I didn't fully understand it at the time. Twenty-three-year olds aren't exactly known for their deep comprehension of life issues. Although you couldn't have convinced me of that fact when I was twenty-three." He shifted his lower jaw sideways for an instant. "The other reason is because I've never talked about this stuff. But I'm going to start."

"You are." It was a flat statement, edged with a minor amount of disbelief.

"Bottling it up didn't help anything." His expression softened as their gazes connected and his hand slid over her leg. "I was protective of my dad; sorry for how his life had turned out. I wanted to win for him, but in a way... his needing Austin and me to win so badly... made him seem kind of weak." His mouth tightened ever so slightly. "Does that make sense?"

"Yes. It does." Perfect sense.

"When I was torn as to whether or not to go all out professionally, try to make the NFR Finals, he said that whatever I left behind would be waiting when I got back."

"Was he referring to me?"

"Probably."

She shot him a sideways look. "You know… that kind of makes me mad."

"That he said it, or that I believed it?"

"Both?"

"I was afraid of becoming my dad, Shelby, and I was worried about you becoming like my mom, controlled by her husband's resentment. I believed Dad when he said I needed to follow my dreams. Both Austin and I did."

"So you left me."

"I asked you to come, despite my dad telling me not to."

"I felt like my dream was taking second place to yours."

"I thought that my dream had a time limit and yours didn't."

She frowned over at him. "I wish we could have said these things four years ago."

His grip on her thigh tightened ever so slightly. "Maybe we needed four years to think."

"Why the confession now, Ty?"

"Because if we are going to try to build something, we need to truly understand where we stand. What our fears and motivations are. We loved each other before, but we didn't share a lot." He paused for a moment and then said, "My riding scares you, doesn't it?"

Shelby looked down at her lap and was surprised to see

that she was twisting her hands together. She released her fingers and laid her palms on her thighs, splaying the fingers. "I may as well just come out and say it. Yes. Your riding scares me."

"So why did you tell me to ride tonight?"

"I think you should do this documentary. It's a huge deal. My fear of your riding... that's my problem. Not yours."

"No. It's our problem." She looked up at him and he smoothed the hair back from her cheek with a gentle stroke of his hand. "I'm not leaving you, Shelby. Whether or not I ride, I'm not leaving you."

"You can't promise that. Look at what happened to Harry."

There. She'd said it. Let out her biggest fear. Losing Ty permanently.

"And your mom."

Shelby swallowed. "And my mom."

Ty leaned in and kissed her then. A sweet, I'm-there-for-you kiss, his lips moving gently over hers, one hand cradling the back of her head, the other at her cheek. As he pulled back, Shelby opened her eyes and focused on the man sitting a few inches away from her, whose taste was still on her lips. A man she couldn't stand to lose again.

"Maybe we should go home," she whispered. "We can get my truck in the morning."

"Good idea."

Chapter Fourteen

SHELBY AND TY didn't talk as he took the back roads home to the Forty-Six Ranch, but there wasn't much more that needed said. What Shelby needed now was time to process.

She called the hospital shortly after arriving home and was told her grandfather was doing well and, if nothing changed, she'd be able to pick him up at noon the following day. Shortly after that, she called the insurance company, the salvage company that had towed Gramps's truck, and Cassie, just to let her know that all was essentially well.

"Do you want to stay with me? Or do you want me to come to the ranch?" Cassie asked. "Because you shouldn't be alone right now."

"I'm not alone," Shelby said simply. Ty was outside feeding and she knew he wasn't going anywhere. "I'll talk to you tomorrow."

She ended the call and set the phone on the table. It would be twilight soon. What had been one of the longest days of her adult life was almost over.

And she was not alone.

That meant so much. She could have handled alone, because she was a survivor, but she didn't want to. She wanted to be with Ty. She wanted to wake up in the morning with him there next to her, and go to sleep at night curled up against him. And she wanted him to follow the dream that meant so much to him.

Shelby got to her feet and walked out the door, the crisp, early evening breeze ruffling her hair. She spotted Ty near the homestead house and started toward him. His head lifted as she approached.

"Come to the house. I'll zap something for dinner."

"Zapped food is my favorite."

She smiled a little and started back the way she came. Ty caught up with her, slipped his thumb under the top of her belt as he brought an arm around her, making her jeans ride lower on one side.

"You know I hate that."

"Uh huh."

She didn't hate it. She loved the familiarity of it. Loved this fragile bubble around them. Was he staying or going? They had to talk. For real. But she wasn't ready yet. She understood so much more than she had before. She'd accused him of not talking, but now he had.

The ball was firmly in her court.

Once they reached the house, Ty pulled dishes out of the cupboard as she microwaved a tray of frozen lasagna. She was not hungry, but Ty had to be, and she'd eat with him.

Once the food was on the table, though, she discovered she was ravenous. Her grandfather was okay and the guy she totally loved was here with her.

"Do you want to talk?" Ty asked after they'd finished the dishes. Shelby shook her head.

She snapped off the kitchen light and reached out to take his hand in hers, loving the feel of his work-roughened skin against hers. "Don't want to talk." She led him down the hall to her room, pausing outside the door to say, "But I wouldn't mind another kind of communication."

He leaned down to touch her forehead with his, his breath warm on her face as he said, "I'm your guy."

A tingle went up Shelby's spine. He was her guy.

She opened the door and led him inside. Shadows stretched across the room, but Shelby didn't bother with the lights. She reached out for her guy, smoothed her hands over his hard chest, then undid the buttons of his shirt one by one, focusing on how much she loved touching him, running her hands over his skin, feeling his response. She pulled the shirt tails out and then pushed the shirt off his shoulders. Leaning in she traced the muscles of his chest with her lips. He tasted of salt and dust and man. She loved it.

His hands fisted in her hair and he tilted her face up. "I need a shower."

"So do I."

Shelby slowly washed every inch of Ty's muscled body,

memorizing it yet again. He returned the favor, and then they kissed as they rinsed off, Shelby's hand firmly gripping his erection which was pressed between their bellies.

After toweling off, she went to her knees, taking him in her mouth as he stroked the damp hair away from the sides of her face. She brought him close, then pulled back and he helped her to her feet, then swung her up into his arms and carried her to the dark bedroom where their clothing lay in tangles on the floor. He laid her down, and then, after a melting kiss, moved his lips down her neck to her breasts, making her arch and gasp. He smiled against her belly, his stubble rough against her delicate skin, then continued his sensual journey south. As he touched his tongue to her sex, she jerked, then relaxed and let her eyes drift shut as he did that thing he did so well, teasing her clit with his fingers and his tongue. She gave another gasp, then pulled her hips back, breaking the delicious contact as she came too, too close to going over the edge. Ty looked up at her and she reached down to take hold of his shoulders, pull him up to where he belonged—on her, in her. As he eased his way inside of her, Shelby pressed her face against the hollow of his shoulder, closed her eyes, breathed in his scent. He was part of her.

They made love slowly, savoring the closeness, the familiarity and the uncertainty. Shelby had no idea what the future held, but she had Ty with her *now*. It was the now that mattered. She'd deal with the future later, when she could think, because her thoughts were tangling as her need for release grew. And then she was hanging on, taking everything Ty had to give and giving back all she could.

The orgasm rocked her and she gave a sobbing gasp before biting down on his shoulder. Ty came the instant her teeth hit flesh, shoving into her one last time before holding and then finally, as if drained of every ounce of strength, collapsing onto his side, pulling her with him so that they were still joined.

Shelby hugged him close, pressing her face against his damp chest.

She loved this man so damned much.

TY AWOKE AT sunrise like usual, only he didn't get out of bed. Instead he rolled over and woke Shelby in the best way he knew how. She seemed appreciative.

"If you make the coffee, I'll see about breakfast," she said when she finally eased herself out of his embrace and slid out of bed, pausing long enough to kiss his bruised shoulder.

"I'm good with coffee." He swung his legs over the edge of the bed and stretched. He was sore. Yesterday's ride had been killer, but he was grateful to his dad and Buck for making it possible, because it could well be his last ride.

Fifteen minutes later they were sitting on the weathered porch, watching the sun top the trees. Sitting in the morning silence, feeling this woman next to him... things were as perfect as it could get, given the circumstances. They still had to get Les home and strong arm him into taking care of himself, and Ty had to settle issues with his dad. But he was on the right track there, reclaiming his life. He leaned into Shelby, who pressed back against him. Another old game they used to play. It was so damned easy to fall back into things with her. He knew now that when he'd come back, he hadn't needed closure. He'd needed to acknowledge all the shit he'd kept buried inside. As had she. Who knew?

He gave his head a small shake.

"What?" Shelby asked.

"We're so damned lucky."

"How so?"

He turned his head to frown at her. "Do you know easily we could have *not* been here right now?"

"So this is where you want to be?"

"I had a stellar last ride and that was a gift. I'm good." He pulled in a breath that swelled his chest and slowly exhaled as he stared out over the pasture where the horses were grazing. "But even if I had left, I would have found my way back to you. Then I would have hammered at your defenses until you let me back into your life."

"I have pretty good defenses."

He gave a small snort. "No kidding." He was quiet for a moment. "I think maybe things had to play out this way."

Shelby pulled away from him, so their shoulders no longer touched. "In some ways, I love watching you ride."

He frowned. "I thought it scared you."

"It does. But... there's another aspect to it—something about watching you do something that you so clearly love, and that you're so damned good at. It's... I don't know... thrilling, maybe?"

He smiled a little. "I thrill you?"

She smiled back, a wry curve of her lips. "In many ways."

He breathed deeply and stared back out over the pastures, still smiling a little.

"I want you to go back out on the road." His gaze jerked back to hers, before he could speak, she said, "Your dad was right. If you quit before you're finished, the unanswered question will always be there... could you have done it again?"

"Maybe I don't need an answer."

"Maybe I do." She put her hand on his leg. "I need you to do this... and I need to be there for it."

"You want to go with me?"

"I need to face my fears. It's part of life, facing fears. I'd never feel right dodging this." Her expression grew fierce. "I can do this. What is it? Eight seconds once a week? And think of all the time we'd have in between those eight-second rides."

"I... uh..."

Shelby took his face in her hands. "I thought about this last night. For a long time. I can be done with my contracts in less than three weeks. It's getting close to the time of year when I don't take on any more horses. I can get Cass and

Jess to keep an eye on Gramps… Jess has been looking for another place to live anyway."

"Maybe he'd like Hawksley's trailer."

She smiled innocently. "I thought we could take it with us. Live in it."

"Oh, hell no. That thing will rip to pieces if it traveled too fast and far… which is exactly what we will be doing." He slid his hand around the back of her neck, pulling her closer. "I thought last night, when you talked about me doing the documentary, you were doing the brave thing. You know, tossing it out there as a kind of peace offering."

"No. You were right about the need to understand one another so that we can build together. I understand that you would stay, but I understand that you need to ride, too. We can't pass up an opportunity like this, Ty." She leaned forward to first kiss him, then nip his lower lip. "Let's go make a documentary."

His hand tightened at the back of her neck. She was sure about her decision. He knew her well enough to be certain of that. "We can bail at any time. It'll make Buck's movie all the more dramatic."

She brought her hands up to his shoulders and gave him a small shake. "We're not bailing."

The phone rang in the house and Shelby got to her feet, hurrying into the house to answer it. Ty waited where he was, sorting through her amazing offer. When she came back, she was smiling.

"Hospital?" he asked.

"Gramps himself. He'd like to get out of that 'hell hole' ASAP."

"And the hospital? How do they feel about it?"

"According to Gramps, he can be released at noon, but he has appointments for testing with Dr. Murphy early this week."

"He's going to be a handful when he gets home."

"Understatement of the year."

"You're sure you can leave him?"

"Here's what I am sure of... the three of us can work things out. Compromise. And no matter what, when this next rodeo season ends, we'll be together. That's the important thing.

Ty leaned forward to kiss the woman he loved. "Actually, babe, it's the only thing."

Epilogue

"**A**RE THINGS ANY better?" Shelby came by to perch on the arm of Ty's chair after he hung up the phone. His dad was driving him nuts, but he was also trying very, very hard to accept the fact that even though, seven months in, Ty was having a stellar comeback season, sitting fifth in the standings, this was his last rodeo season.

"He only dropped a couple of heavy hints about guys still competing that were way older than I am." Ty smiled up at her. "He asked about you, though. And Les."

Which meant he was trying to accept Ty's choices in life—and the small fact that Ty's life was his own to live as he saw fit. It also meant his dad was probably driving Austin crazy, but Austin was so much better suited to fend off their fathers' interfering ways without offending the old man. That was how it was when one took very little in life, except for their career, seriously.

"So I'm no longer the wench that's stealing you away from rodeo."

Ty pulled her down into his lap. "No. You're still totally

that."

"Hey. Hey. None of that." Les came into the living room carrying a mug of tea and a plate of cookies and scowled at them. But his scowl wasn't as deadly as it'd been a little over half a year ago, when Ty had first started helping him fence. "Yours is poured, but you got to get it yourself."

"I'll go." Shelby maneuvered herself off Ty's lap and headed for the kitchen. "You took your meds, right?" she called back to Les.

"Jess has me well trained," he replied before lifting his tea mug and taking a small sip.

The guy had been a godsend. After moving into the trailer, Jess had used his carpentry talents to totally refurbish it, with Callen's permission, and what had once been a ratty tin can was now a funky showpiece. And somehow he'd managed to put Les on a meds schedule and help around the place on weekends.

Ty heard the spoon rattle in the sugar bowl as Shelby fixed the tea, and waited for the question that came almost every time he and Shelby managed to make it home for a few days between rodeos. When was he going to make an honest woman of Shelby?

"So," Les said gruffly. "When—"

"November."

Les's eyes bugged a little. "You aren't kidding an old man."

"Wouldn't dream of it." He made a gesture rather than

finish his sentence as Shelby came in carrying the tea.

She stopped dead when she saw the expression on Les's face. "You told him."

"He asked."

Shelby set down the tea mugs. "Are you okay with this?" she asked her grandfather. "I know we've only been seriously together for a short time—"

"You've been together a lot longer than that," Les muttered gruffly. "And yeah. I'm okay with this."

"Will you come to Vegas with us for the wedding?" Shelby settled once again on the arm of Ty's chair.

"Vegas?"

"We're getting married just before the National Finals," Ty said. "That way, no matter what happens there, I'm a winner." Even if he got injured before the season was over and wasn't able to qualify, he'd be a winner.

A slow smile built on Les's lined face. "Yeah. Good thinking." He frowned suddenly. "Won't be an Elvis wedding, will it? Because I don't know if I can give my granddaughter away at an Elvis wedding."

"Low-key cowboy wedding. Buck asked about filming it, but we said no. He can get some footage afterward. And Shelby's agreed to do some talking on camera about life the road." As well as facing fears.

As the months had passed, her anxiety had subsided—to the point she was now analyzing Ty's rides with him. Buck, being the student of human nature he was, had watched her transformation and now wanted her interview as part of his documentary. It seemed like the least they could do for the guy who'd hired Ty to cover the Idaho, Montana, and Wyoming rodeo circuits for *Rough Stock World* after his official retirement in December.

Once his season was over, Shelby would take up training again at the Forty-Six and when Ty wasn't covering the rodeos, he'd work the ranch. They wouldn't get rich, but that had never been his goal. All he'd ever wanted was a life with no regrets. He settled his hand on Shelby's thigh.

There was just that one small thing…

"Are you sure you want to buy that gelding? They want too much money."

She gave him a look. "Evarado and I understand one another. This is the perfect solution for everyone. Paul can pretend I fell in love with him and couldn't let him go, and he can use the money to buy Blake a pretty horse that she can handle. I found one today that might be perfect for her."

"Stubborn woman."

She clinked her tea mug against his. "Stubborn man." She leaned in to kiss him lightly. "Thank goodness."

The End

If you enjoyed *Catch Me, Cowboy*, you'll love…

The 78th Copper Mountain Rodeo Series

Book 1: Catch Me, Cowboy by Jeannie Watt

Book 2: Protect Me, Cowboy by Shelli Stevens

Book 3: Want Me, Cowboy by Sinclair Jayne

Book 4: Love Me, Cowgirl by Eve Gaddy

More books by Jeannie Watt

The Montana Bride

The Jackson Family Legacy series

The Christmas Secret

The Jackson Family Legacy series

Available now at your favorite online retailer!

About the Author

Jeannie Watt is the author of over 20 contemporary romances and the recipient of the Holt Medallion Award of Merit. She lives in a small ranching community—a place where kids really do grow up to be cowboys—with her husband, dog, cat, horses and ponies. When she's not writing, Jeannie enjoys sewing retro fashions, running, and buying lots and lots of hay.

If you'd like to know more about Jeannie, check out her website JeannieWatt.com.

Thank you for reading

Catch Me, Cowboy

If you enjoyed this book, you can find more from all our great authors at TulePublishing.com, or from your favorite online retailer.

TULE
PUBLISHING

.

Printed in Great Britain
by Amazon